www.therealchencia.com

Editing: Little Pear Editing

AN ILLICIT SEDUCTION

A DARK EROTIC EXPERIENCE

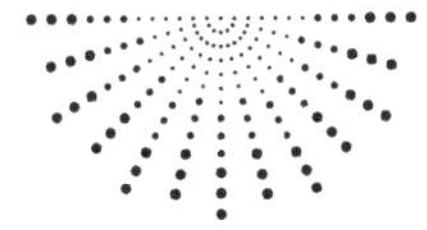

CHENCIA C. HIGGINS

EKOL MEDIA

ALSO BY CHENCIA C. HIGGINS

JustOneNight.com Novella Series:

No Strings Allowed - Book 1

No Love Allowed - Book 2

The Week Before Forever – Book 2.5

No Games Allowed - Book 3

Holiday Honey – Book 4

K.S.L. – Book 5

The Vow Series:

To Buy a Vow – Book 1

To Build a Vow – Book 2

To Break a Vow – Book 3

Things Hoped For – Book 4

Wolves of West Texas Series:

Janine: His True Alpha – Book 1

Lenora: His Omega Mate – Book 2

Alicia: His Troublesome Fate – Book 3

The Color Spectrum Duet:

The Color Spectrum: Ebony

<u>Black Family Saga:</u>

Glasses

Fast Breaker

<u>The Luminous Cruse Chronicles:</u>

Love On The Luminous

<u>Boos & Booze</u>

Costume Cutty

<u>Standalones:</u>

Her & Them

Remember Our Love

Loud & Lew'd

Benefriends

An Illicit Seduction

Consolation Gifts

"I can't even see straight until I've had my face in between your legs."

After a night of heavy drinking with her coworkers, Seraph succumbs to an erotic dream in which she experiences unbridled pleasure beyond her wildest imagination. It's a brand of filth that she enjoys but is undoubtedly wrong, though she can't rationalize why. What she does know is that she can't deny how euphoric it feels and that she may not want it to stop.

When she awakens mid-climax, she comes face-to-face with a nightmare that she can't escape. At every turn, he's there and won't take no for an answer. As she is relentlessly pursued, her defenses crumble until she surrenders in defeat—just as he intended.

An Illicit Seduction is not a romance. It is not a love story with a guaranteed happily ever after. It is a dark, erotic tale intended for mature readers at least 18+ and contains taboo themes, explicitly non-consensual sex scenes, and strong language.

Oh, and a little voodoo too.

1

THE BEFORE

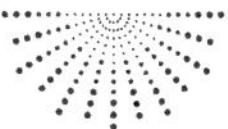

"HEY, SERAPH. DO YOU HAVE A MINUTE?"

Looking up from the spreadsheets covering the surface of her desk, Seraph twisted in her chair to face the woman standing in the doorway of her office. She pushed her thick passion twists out of her face, flicking the ends over her shoulder, and smiled. "Sure, what's up?"

Jaime settled into one of the chairs in front of Seraph's desk and sat forward. "Well, as you know, my annual pajama party is coming up, and I was thinking about inviting Damon."

Seraph nodded, hoping that Jaime didn't think she needed to ask her permission to extend the invitation. "I'm sure he'd love it." She didn't know a man who wouldn't.

Jaime nodded. "Right. Well, the thing is he's so

quiet that I haven't really had a chance to talk to him, and I was wondering if you could just bring him with you."

Tilting her head as if she didn't understand the question, Seraph observed the woman whom she'd worked with for over twelve years. This was an uncharacteristic request. Jaime had such a bold personality that she rarely met a person who didn't immediately fall under her spell, so this hesitance threw her for a loop. And—not that Jaime would know—asking Damon to attend a party like Jaime's Pajama Jam with her would be awkward as hell.

"I don't understand how his being quiet would keep you from inviting him…" she trailed off as a sheepish look crept onto Jaime's face and a light bulb clicked on. Seraph laughed, shaking her head at her coworker and friend. "Oh my gosh! You *like* him. Is that why you're in here with this crappy excuse?"

Covering her face, Jaime giggled as she nodded, her wash and go curls bobbing with each movement. "Yessss. He's so fine I can't stand it, and those damn dimples get me every time!"

Jaime's voice had taken on a high-pitched tone, and her tawny cheeks were tinged pink at her revelation. Seraph was tickled by her reaction. Jaime had a new office crush every other month, and it was hilarious that Damon was the latest object of her affection. Jaime had started with the company the same year as Seraph, but while Seraph was an account manager in the sales department, Jaime was an event coordinator from marketing, and she excelled at her position. A couple of years younger than Seraph's thirty-six, Jaime had come to the company straight out of undergrad and started as a receptionist, eventually working her way up the corporate ladder.

"That still doesn't explain why you're telling me how you're thinking about inviting him instead of just…inviting him."

"Oh! Well, I wanted to run it by you first…just to make sure I wasn't stepping on any toes."

"Stepping on toes?" she repeated, confused by Jaime's words. What in the world did *that* mean?

Fake-pouting, Jaime asked, "You're going to make me say it?"

Seraph shrugged her shoulders. "I'm afraid so; I have no idea what you're talking about."

Jaime sighed then licked her lips. "Well, I kind of assumed that you two might have something going on…"

Seraph's eyes ballooned as Jaime's meaning hit her. Then, she began shaking her head emphatically. "What?! Girl, no. We do not—are not—we're just—" She stopped talking before she could say too much.

Laughing a little at herself, she rolled her eyes and made eye contact with Jaime. "Damon and I do not have anything going on. There are no toes to step on over here."

Jaime eyed her skeptically, and Seraph wondered what, if anything, had Damon been saying that this was even on anyone's mind. He had been a programmer for the company for maybe three months, but their departments didn't interact at all, so they barely saw each other. They occasionally had lunch together but always opted for an off-site restaurant instead of the cafe in the lobby of their building. Seraph knew the few minutes of them walking to and from the elevator didn't give off any romantic vibes. It couldn't. So, what was going on?

"Are you sure? If that's you, I won't mind—hell, I'd understand!"

Seraph's laugh was loud in the small room that felt larger than it was because of the wall of windows on her left. "Jaime. *Girl.* No. I've watched him play video games for hours with a pair of underwear on his head. I can promise you that I am not in the way of whatever you want to pursue with him."

For anyone else, this would have been the weirdest conversation they'd ever had, hands down, but for Seraph, this was just a regular Tuesday. Damon drew attention and whenever Seraph was with him, women felt bold enough to ask *her* about him. She figured that was usually because they could tell that he wasn't her man. This particular incident was a new one, but the sentiment was the same.

There was a short knock on her door before it swung open to reveal the very man they were discussing. *Speak of the devil,* she thought as she raised her brows in question. It didn't take much thought to deduce the reason he'd come to her office, but after Jaime's questions—and skepticism—Seraph was wary of how things between them came off.

With just one look, it was clear why Jaime—and many other women around the office—wanted him. With his smooth, sepia-toned skin, perfectly round bald head and connecting beard and mustache, he was pure perfection. Add in cavernous dimples that only appeared when he smiled, thick thighs, and a strong back, Damon was the literal existence of fantasies. Seraph could objectively agree that Damon was attractive, but she still couldn't reconcile his current grown man status with the little boy she had known since she was a teenager.

It didn't help that when she left for college, Damon was nine-years-old, but when Seraph returned six years later, he was nowhere to be found, having gone to live with his mother in Dallas. He'd attended high school in Dallas and then immediately left for a local university in that area. Seraph didn't see him again until he was twenty-three when she ran into him at her mother's house on a random Saturday. That was four years ago, and she hadn't seen him consistently until he relocated back to Houston shortly before he started working for Seraph's company. It was only recently that she began seeing him regularly and that was because they worked together. She didn't witness his rise to adolescence and puberty, so her brain still held on to the image of him as a nine-year-old.

"Sorry for interrupting."

Damon's low voice pulled her out of her thoughts, and Seraph shook her head and smiled. "It's alright. How can I help you?"

"I—uh," his eyes flickered from Seraph to Jaime then back to Seraph. "I stopped by to see if you wanted to join me for lunch…but it looks like you're busy, so—"

"Hey, Damon," Jaime cooed, looking back and forth between him and Seraph.

Seraph pursed her lips at the knowing look that Jaime was aiming her way. Jaime didn't know anything and had been far off base, but this didn't help make Seraph's case. Any other day, she would have agreed without hesitation, but since Jaime was present—and currently staring an eager hole into the side of her face—she simply gave Damon an apologetic smile.

"Thanks for the offer, Damon, but unfortunately, I have a previous engagement for lunch." Jaime quirked an eyebrow, and Seraph bit her lip to keep from laughing out loud.

"Oh, but hey! Jaime's free. Why don't the two of you go to lunch instead?" Seraph pasted a wide smile on her face and took in each of their expressions. Jaime had a hopeful grin on her face, but Damon looked dumbfounded. "It will give you guys a chance to get to know each other better, and Jaime can tell you all about the Pajama Jam at the end of the month."

Damon shoved his hands into the pockets of his slacks. "Pajama Jam?"

Seraph nodded and shuffled the papers around on her desk, studiously ignoring the disappointment on his face.

"Yeah," Jaime added. "It's an annual party I throw every year for the grown and sexy. You've got the sexy part down, but why don't we go to that Mexican place around the corner and you let me decide if you're grown enough?"

He laughed and those dimples sprang out, causing Jaime to fan herself with her hand.

At Jaime's theatrics, Seraph stood and shooed the

both of them out of her office and waved them off before closing her door and sighing with relief.

Playing matchmaker wasn't her favorite role, but what harm could come from helping two single people to let nature take its course?

2

THE BRUNCH

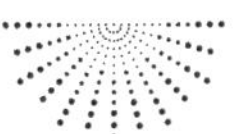

AT LEAST ONE SUNDAY A MONTH, SERAPH AND HER TRIO of best friends Vanessa, Sierra, and Twyla set aside a few hours in their busy schedules to get together and relax. They temporarily suppressed the stress from their careers, significant others, and other demands of their time to enjoy a good meal and great conversation. This particular Sunday found them at Lakeside Lounge in Fourth Ward. There had been a forty-five-minute wait for a table, but according to the reviews, the wait was worth it. The seafood-themed menu never disappointed; the drinks were top shelf—and bottomless—and the DJ knew his way around a set of turntables. The four women bopped in their seats as they placed their orders for appetizers and bottomless mimosas.

Twyla was the first to speak after sipping on the

water that the server had delivered as soon as they sat down. "Lord, y'all don't even know how bad I needed this outing."

"Work stressing you out that much?" Vanessa asked.

Nodding, Twyla cringed. "Worse."

Seraph frowned. Twyla was a kindergarten teacher at Bright Horizons, a prestigious, private elementary school, and although it seemed like a place that would have fewer issues than a public institution, according to Twyla—who had attended both public and private schools growing up—the rich folks were the most difficult to deal with.

"Is it the kids or the parents this time?"

"The parents," she replied quickly. "Always the parents."

She paused as the server placed a pitcher of pineapple mimosas and a basket of crawfish-stuffed cornbread muffins on the table. He took everyone's meal order and disappeared, quickly weaving through the bistro-style tables and pub chairs that filled the center of the restaurant's dining room. Along the perimeter of the room, perched on wooden platforms, were half-moon booths wide enough to house at least six adults, and through a set of opened French doors, half a dozen cabanas outfitted with turquoise cushions and umbrellas could be seen on the back patio. With the warm spring breeze filtering in through the open doors on either side of the restaurant and high-energy hip-hop beats to keep its patrons rocking in their seats, Lakeside Lounge was the perfect place for a late morning outing.

As the women chatted and enjoyed their drinks and appetizers, their server delivered their meals in less than twenty minutes, and the conversation shifted from work stress to appreciation for their food while they ate. Seraph was attacking her wild gulf shrimp and smoked Gouda grits with gusto when Sierra tapped her arm to get her attention.

"Hey, isn't that Damon?"

Directing her gaze to Sierra's pointed stiletto nails, Seraph twisted around in her seat and craned her neck toward the front of the restaurant. Sure enough, it was Damon. He stood near the host podium in a cluster with five other men. There was a slight grin on his face as he shook his head while the other men laughed. They were all dressed accordingly as Lakeside had a strict no denim or leisurewear policy, and Seraph was impressed that there wasn't one tennis shoe in the bunch. When her neck began to strain, she returned to face her friends.

"Yeah, that's him."

"How long has he been back?" Vanessa asked as

she peeled open a large crawfish and popped the juicy tail meat in her mouth.

Seraph's eyebrows met contemplatively as she tried to remember. "About six months, I think."

"How's he doing at NexTech?"

"Really well. His department manager stopped by after a meeting last month and thanked me again for referring him. He said that Damon is a natural at programming and has made his job less stressful."

"Aww," Sierra sang, "that's so sweet. I'm glad it's working out for him."

Swallowing a mouthful of grits, Seraph nodded. "Me too."

Their server stopped by and dropped off a fresh pitcher of mimosas as if on cue, and Seraph quickly refilled her glass before digging back into her bowl. She was sucking the savory, spicy sauce from the shrimp off of one of her fingers when Sierra called her name.

"Huh?"

"You're not going to wave to him or anything?"

She frowned and shook her head. "I'm eating, SiSi. I can say hey to him at any time." Returning her attention back to her food, she felt Sierra's stare as she picked up her spoon and scooped a mound of grits into her mouth. Glancing at her, she noticed Sierra's pursed lips and rolled her eyes playfully.

Catching on to the exchange, Twyla shook her head, and her pink-painted lips curved into an amused grin.

Sierra pouted. "Shit. I was hoping your ass would be sociable today so I can get a better look at his fine ass."

The other three women erupted into laughter and Sierra joined in.

"I'm serious!"

Rolling her eyes again, Seraph pointed her empty spoon at the woman who—along with Vanessa—had been one of her closest friends since they met in college more than fifteen years ago. "Am I not enjoying a social meal with my girlfriends?"

Swiping her auburn, asymmetrical bangs from her eyes, Sierra gave Seraph a look that clearly said *duh*. "Well, yeah, but I want you to be *extra* sociable for two minutes so I can devour some eye candy up close and personal-like." Her eyes flicked over Seraph's shoulder again and she made a satisfied clucking sound in the back of her throat. "Hell, his friends look fine too. Matter of fact, call all of those niggas over!"

"Damn, SiSi!" Twyla giggled. She had joined their trio five years earlier after meeting Vanessa and hitting it off at a gym that catered to plus-size women. Even though she was a few years younger than the other three, she fit in as if she was the long-lost fourth member to their Destiny's Child. "What does Devin think about your eye candy addiction?"

Sierra frowned, and Seraph joined in on Twyla's laughter.

"Ask her again, T."

"Man, whatever. *My man* doesn't mind me looking because he knows that's all it is. Besides," she added, shooting a sly look over to Seraph before picking up her glass and bringing it to her lips, "it's not like Damon would be interested even if I *was* checking for him like that. We *all* know who he wants."

"Oop!" Vanessa's eyes bucked and she rolled her lips into her mouth to stave off a laugh.

Seraph narrowed her eyes, and all four women sat in silence, two sets of eyes bouncing between her and Sierra before the two of them simultaneously burst into laughter.

"You tried it, bitch."

"Tried to set the truth free," Sierra murmured under her breath, and although Seraph heard her, she let the slick comment go without acknowledgment.

They let the conversation drop and resumed eating, but a moment later, the tapping of Vanessa's long, acrylic nails on the glazed, wooden tabletop grabbed their attention.

"Aww," she trilled, "SiSi look! Ask and you shall receive. He's coming over here!"

Bending her neck, Seraph gave the bowl in front of her every bit of her attention as if its last vestiges had morphed from a simple southern staple into a puzzle she needed to decode to save the world from mass destruction. Not even thirty seconds later, she felt him behind her at the same time that Sierra kicked her foot under the table. He came to a stop at her side, his hand gripping the back of her chair in a way that caused his thumb to press into her back. His presence was neither overwhelming nor unpleasant, but the heat from that thumb touching a tiny sliver of her skin that was exposed, thanks to her open-back top, caused a funny sensation to crop up in her belly, and she didn't know whether to lean away from it or lean into it. She swallowed hard at the indecision.

"*Hey, Damon!*" Sierra, Vanessa, and Twyla all chirped at once, sounding like a hell-bound choir of old thirst-buckets.

"What's up, ladies?" Damon greeted politely then curved his head and dropped his eyes to the side of Seraph's face. "Hey, Seraph."

At the sound of her name being spoken in that low, melodic baritone, Seraph's eyelids fluttered and she wiped her mouth with her napkin before looking up at him with a friendly smile. Although she was annoyed by her friend's comments, she had no desire to take it out on him by being unnecessarily rude. "Hi, Damon. You're looking mighty dapper this fine afternoon."

Beneath his neat mustache, a pleased smile lit up his deep brown face, putting his prominent dimples on display. He wore a short-sleeved, red polo that was tucked into a pair of light-gray chinos that stopped just below his bare ankles. On his sockless feet were red boat shoes that paired well with the nautical theme of the restaurant.

"Thank you. You look striking…as always. This yellow blouse makes your skin glow."

Seraph smiled in return. One thing about Damon was that he took his attire very seriously, and whenever Seraph saw him, she made it a point to tell him that his efforts paid off. It was second nature for her to compliment him, and he always reciprocated. Their exchanges always seemed innocent enough, but with her girlfriends witnessing it firsthand, she felt a little awkward, which was happening more often, and she wished for a way to make it stop. When he touched two of her twists and moved them off of her shoulder, she chewed on the corner of her lip to hide her sudden, sharp intake of breath and reached for her glass.

Thankfully, Damon seemed to read the moment

well enough. He removed his hand from the back of her chair, lightly trailing his fingertips along her back, inciting a full-body shiver in Seraph, and took a step back.

"Well, I'll let you all get back to your meal. See you later, Seraph." With a nod, he turned and walked toward the back of the restaurant where the host had led his group of friends.

Once he disappeared around the corner of the restaurant, all three of Seraph's friends began speaking at once as she threw back her glass and drained the last of her drink.

"That is one fine man!"

"Ooh girl, he wants you *bad*!"

"Aww, y'all are so cute!"

Shaking her head, she grabbed the pitcher and refilled her glass once more. "All three of you are fucking insane."

Twyla leaned toward her. "Don't be like that, friend."

Seraph glared at Twyla. "You're trying to get me sent to hell like I haven't been busting my ass to earn my way back into heaven after those wild years in undergrad!"

Sierra bucked her eyes and jerked her neck back. "With all of the shit you did, there isn't enough redemption in the Gulf of Mexico! You might as well hop on Damon's dick and ride that nigga to the seventh level of hell!"

Twyla screamed and Vanessa burst out laughing, spraying chewed bits of crawfish across the table.

"Oh my god!" Vanessa yelled, laughter and the food in her mouth making her words barely decipherable. "My bad, y'all!"

Shaking her head and trying valiantly not to laugh herself, Seraph pushed back from the table. "I'm going to the bathroom. You bitches have turned my stomach."

The three women laughed even louder as Seraph waved her middle finger at them and walked off. After washing her hands and rearranging her twists in the mirror, she exited the bathroom just as Damon came through the door that separated the hallway from the rest of the restaurant. Maybe, it was all of the comments from her friends or maybe, it was the influence of the six mimosas she'd imbibed, but suddenly she couldn't help but notice the way his feet turned out as he walked and the way his shirt stretched across his shoulders and hugged his chest. *Were those his nipples?*

Yeah, it was definitely the mimosas.

Putting those dimples on display, Damon smiled at her. "I saw your friends packing up on my way back here. What are y'all about to get into?"

Seraph shrugged. "I'm not sure. Twyla mentioned something about a new exhibit at the fine arts museum, so we might head there."

"Oh yeah? I love the MOFA. Let me know when y'all decide, and I can come through."

She pursed her lips. "You're just gonna abandon your boys like that?"

He stared at her for a moment, not uttering a word and just letting his eyes roam her entire length before he bit his lip, his grin widening.

"I think they'd understand."

Her breath caught in her throat, and she thought about the way his fingers had trailed up her back not even ten minutes earlier. She shook her head and averted her eyes, glancing behind him at the door that muffled the loud noise from the dining room of the restaurant.

"Don't look at me like that, Damon."

His brows lifted and he brushed his palm down and over his mustache. He dropped his gaze to the ground before lifting it back up to her, something akin to determination glinting in his dark-brown depths. "How am I looking at you?"

A dozen thoughts ran through her head, all battling to exit her mouth first.

"Like you don't know me like you know me. Like, I'm some woman you just met. Like, you want m—" Breaking off on a chuckle, Seraph shook her head. She was going to need a gallon of water to clear her head if this was how the mimosas had her. Those damn drinks almost had some wild shit about to come out of her mouth. "You know what? I'm tripping. I need to go. I'll see you later." She started toward him, stopping within arm's reach when he didn't move. Hesitantly, she tilted her head back until they were face-to-face.

"May I pass?"

"Yeah. Are you going to shoot me the info about the museum?"

"Hell no! This is my free time with my girls. I'm not about to ruin it by having to babysit your ass, and I refuse to watch you spend the time all up in their faces."

One thick eyebrow lifted into the air. "Babysit me?"

"You heard me."

Dimples disappearing as his once jovial smile completely fell from his face, Damon shook his head and moved to one side of the hallway. "Yeah. Alright. See you later."

Seraph nodded and passed by him, being careful not to allow any part of her body to brush his as she hurried back to the dining area.

3
THE PAJAMA JAM

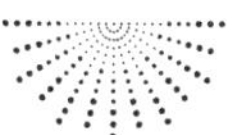

"YOU KNOW THE DRILL. KEYS IN THE BUCKET!"

Seraph grinned at Jaime's silly expression and dropped her rectangular car key into the heart-shaped bucket cradled in her coworker/friend's arms. Jaime was right; after six years of attending the lively—and debaucherous—pajama party she hosted, Seraph definitely knew the drill. It was why she had removed her car key from its packed key ring, dropping the part that held keys to hers and her mother's home into the glove compartment before getting out of her car and walking up the driveway to Jaime's two-story house.

A group of four had walked up behind her and were now waiting to be let in, so Seraph quickly gave Jaime a hug and brushed past her, removing her heavy jacket as she exited the foyer and entered the great room. As she passed under colorful streamers hanging from the entrance, she noticed there was a pile of coats on a chair against the wall. She tossed hers on top of the pile and continued deeper into the room. The party always took place the weekend before Martin Luther King Jr. Day to allow for an extra recovery day, and depending on your "activities", that extra day was a virtual requirement.

Seraph rocked to the nineties R&B that played through hidden speakers as she moved through the room, greeting the few people she recognized from work and smiling at the unfamiliar faces. Although Seraph wasn't late, the party was already in full swing with a cluster of people dancing on the makeshift dance floor where the coffee table would regularly be. Others lounged in metal folding chairs and on the two sofas, engaged in lively conversation while holding plates of food and signature red cups of legendary parties past.

There were people of all shapes, sizes, and hues but a commonality among everyone in attendance was their state of dress. All the partygoers were wearing pajamas. A few people donned goofy onesies featuring popular cartoon characters or animals, but most of the partiers wore nightwear that trended toward sensual. Jaime's party was for the grown and sexy, so Seraph had expected as much, which is why she chose a midnight blue, silk short and matching tank set that she'd purchased specifically for this event. The shorts stopped just below the tops of her thighs and were loose enough that she felt a breeze on her ass cheeks when she walked but fitted enough that she wasn't at risk of them falling off her behind. Her top was loose-fitting like a blouse, with thin spaghetti straps that would have done a terrible job of concealing her nipples if she hadn't chosen to wear a strapless bra to support her breasts. As she observed the other people in the room, she was glad of her decision because even though she was at a pajama party, she did not feel comfortable being completely dressed down as if she was about to get in the bed. This was still a public party full of people—strangers who she didn't socialize with on an intimate level.

Unfortunately, not everyone cared or considered that same sentiment. There were a few women who wore negligees—reminding Seraph of the teddies she'd worn for past lovers—where the hem of the gowns barely brushed the tops of their asses, exposing scantily-clad hind cheeks, and triangles of material on top barely gripped their breasts, hardened nipples, and dark areolas on full, obscene display.

The male attendees, however, were not to be

outdone. Seraph saw at least one man wearing only a pair of tight boxer briefs, which left nothing to the imagination. She bit her lip at the thickness between his legs and thought that maybe that particular image wasn't so unfortunate.

Thankfully, most people were dressed appropriately, like herself. Bopping to the beat of Mary J. Blige's classic hit, Real Love, Seraph danced her way into the kitchen where the center island countertop had been transformed into a buffet. Her stomach rumbled as the enticing aromas called out to her, and she grabbed a plate and began to load it up with the miniature delights that were hidden inside the aluminum trays.

One of Seraph's favorite things about attending Jamie's parties was that, no matter what, she could guarantee that she would always get better than your run-of-the-mill party fare. There was smoked salmon crostini, tiny lump crab cakes, and coconut shrimp kabobs, and she packed her plate with some of everything. She grabbed a second plate for the minced teriyaki steak cradled in boats made of endive leaves, various sushi, and an assortment of fresh fruit, crudités, and accompanying dips. One plate in her hand and the other on the counter, she filled a red cup with some unknown, fruity-smelling concoction labeled Passion Punch when she felt someone press up against her back.

She froze as the unmistakable rod of a hard dick nestled against her covered ass cheeks. For a moment, she stood there, contemplating how she felt and what she wanted to do. She knew what kind of party this was, and she *was* feeling a little frisky. Not to mention, from the feel of things, they were packing some serious heat below the waist. Craning her neck to the side to see who she might be having a little fun with that night, she almost dropped her plate on the floor when she saw that it was Damon standing behind her.

Stomach now churning, she gasped and stepped away from him. "Oh my god! Damon, what the hell are you doing?!

He stared at her, his normally dark brown eyes now nearly black. His full lips curved into a wolfish grin that was borderline sinister. She'd never seen him smile like that before, and it unnerved her. The feeling intensified as he leaned down and smelled her hair. Face scrunched in confusion, she eyed him. He wore a light gray, ribbed tank top and a pair of silk pajama pants in the same shade of blue as her short set, which rode low on his hips. The "v" of his musculature was just barely visible above the waistband of his pants, and she swallowed hard and averted her eyes. She wasn't oblivious; she knew Damon was attractive, but she kept that undisclosed in the deepest recesses of her brain that was never accessed. The replay of his dick pressed against her ass was knocking on the door of that reality and causing her distress.

"I just wanted to see what you had on your plate."

Damon's normally husky voice had taken on an even deeper note that made something slick and hot slither up her spine and caused several warning signs to blare in her head. *What the hell was going on with him?*

Flustered by how weird he was acting and her unfamiliar reaction to him, she copped an attitude. "All you had to do was ask. No need for you to get all up on my back like that. I thought you were some random man that I was going to—" She paused. No need to tell him the lascivious thoughts she'd had before she knew *he* was the one molding himself to her back.

He bit his lip and her thighs quivered. She needed to get away from him, and quickly. This was lust, plain and simple, and he was just an innocent bystander. Once she returned to the great room, she could find someone to work out her sexual frustrations on.

"Yeah," he drawled as he stepped closer to her, "I could have asked, but what would have been the fun in that? Besides, you smell...delicious."

His voice dropped another octave on that last word, and her nerves morphed into concern. This was not the Damon she knew. She would bet all the money in her bank account, and her car, that Damon had already begun drinking and more than likely taken some sort of party drug. From the way he was leering at her, she'd bet it was the new sex drug that she'd heard about. It had similar, euphoric effects to ecstasy but without many of the adverse repercussions. Knowing Damon, he probably took it to help overcome his nerves of being in an unfamiliar crowd and then sought her out for a familiar face just as the effects of the drug began to set in.

"That's just my perfume. I can give you the name of it so you can pick some up for your future girlfriend."

Shaking her head, she walked to the other end of the island and grabbed a napkin even though she already had one tucked up under her plate. Slowly, he walked toward her, and she had the distinct feeling of being hunted.

"What if," he enunciated each word as if they were sentences in their own right, making the moment seem more intense than it should have been, "I only want to smell it on you?"

She gave him a crazy look and laughed. Oh, he was definitely high or drunk—or both.

"Bye, Damon." Lifting her cup in the air, she flicked a pinky at him and walked out of the kitchen to return to the living room. Finding an empty spot on the couch, she sat down and began eating her food, thoughts of that awkward encounter pushed to the back of her mind.

When she was nearly done cleaning her second plate, Jamie plopped down beside her, dressed in a baby doll teddy that had her large breasts pushed damn near up to her throat.

"Girl, you look so cute in that outfit!"

Seraph grinned and struck a pose. "Thank you, I didn't want to hurt 'em too bad, but I had to do a little something, you know?"

Giggling, Jamie nodded and sipped from the cup of punch she held her hands. "Did I ever tell you about that weird lunch that Damon and I went on a couple of weeks ago?

Brows furrowed at Jaime's suddenly serious tone, Seraph shook her head. "No, you never told me anything about it."

Jamie exhaled a gust of air and sank back against the couch. "Girl, it was so weird. First, he wasn't saying anything at all, which I expected because he's always so quiet and shy at the office. I was trying to ask him to go out with me this weekend, but he brushed me off, saying he was going to a bachelor party in New Orleans. I wasn't sweating it, but other than that, he didn't say much at all. I understood that to be his character and knew that going into it, so when I started telling him about the pajama party and he still didn't say a word, it was fine with me." Jaime gave Seraph a look she couldn't decipher. "Until… I mentioned that you would be here."

"Wait, what?" Seraph lowered the salmon crostini from her mouth and gave Jaime her full attention.

Nodding, Jaime pursed her lips and continued. "*Then,* he perked up and started asking me several questions."

"What kind of questions?"

Jaime shrugged. "He wanted to know the attire and asked for suggestions for his own outfit. He… well, he also asked what you would be wearing?"

Seraph's eyes ballooned, and she scooted to the edge of the couch so that she could face Jaime to ensure that she heard her correctly.

"Run that by me one more time."

"Well," Jaime breathed, "he wanted to know what you were wearing. I told him that I didn't know, but it would more than likely be blue since that's your favorite color."

Seraph stared blankly in front of her, conjuring up the image of Damon in those silky pajama bottoms in a shade so similar to her own silk ensemble that all three articles of clothing could have been purchased in one set.

"What the actual fuck is going on?"

She thought she had whispered those words to herself but Jaime clucked her tongue and shifted on the couch beside her.

"Isn't it obvious? He likes you!" She pursed her lips. "And you tried to push me on him!?"

Her top lip curling, Seraph blinked rapidly. "First of all, I did *not* push you on him; you came to me trying to get hooked up. Second of all, there is no way that he likes me. It's impossible."

Jaime's pinched face was the epitome of confusion. "How is it impossible? He's a red-blooded human and you're smart, successful, and gorgeous. Hell, if you weren't straight, I'd have been tried to shoot my shot." She leaned back and ran her gaze up and down the length of Seraph's body. "Shiiiid, a couple more cups of this passion punch and I still might." Her grin was goofy, and although Seraph rolled her eyes, her lips still quirked into a smile.

"Whatever, Jaime."

Giving her a knowing smile, Jaime left it alone. "Mmhmm. Anyways, you know how we get down at the Pajama Jam. He might be a good deal younger than you, but if ever you were going to give him a chance, tonight would be the night."

Even the idea of giving Damon "a chance" to do anything that wasn't platonic caused bile to rise in the back of Seraph's throat. She shook her head. "Not happening."

"Okay, okay. I hear you." Jaime pushed up from the couch and grabbed Seraph's arm, pulling her to stand as well. "Come on. You're done eating, so let's get some more of this passion punch in your system and loosen you up."

Seraph laughed but allowed herself to be tugged toward the kitchen. "I'm half-naked; my ass is two squats from being exposed, and I'm contemplating fucking strangers. I think I'm plenty loose already."

Looking back at her, Jaime grinned, mischief glinting in her sparkling brown eyes. "Once you go from contemplating to executing *then* I'll know you're loose enough."

Despite consuming copious amounts of the passion punch—so named for its natural ability to lower inhibitions—Seraph never made it to the execution stage. Each time she found a worthy candidate, Damon would pop up in her peripheral and she would run off to put some distance between them. His focus seemed magnetized to her, and no matter which common area she tried to lose herself in, he kept finding her, even out on the patio where at least a dozen people were gathered around a couple of hookahs. Too drunk to continue playing mouse to his cat, but not drunk enough to go *there,* Seraph finally retreated to one of Jaime's guest rooms and climbed under the covers of the queen size bed, falling into a deep sleep as soon as her head hit the pillow.

4
DREAM OR NIGHTMARE

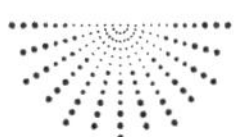

SERAPH WAS BURNING UP.

She was so fucking hot that she felt like a piece of fried chicken sitting under a heat lamp at a buffet. Her body was on fire, and the delicate silk short set now clung to her like armor. No sooner had the thought crossed her mind to shed the now wet fabric that a pair of warm hands gripped the hem of her tank top and rolled the material and her bra up her torso and over her head. Those same hands then pulled her shorts and panties from her body until she lay bare on the bed, but it still wasn't enough. She was combusting from the inside, and if something—some sort of relief—didn't happen soon, she was bound to explode.

Soft lips touched just above her belly button, causing her midsection to concave in surprise and anticipation as the lips traveled up her body until they reached the base of her throat. Opening her eyes, Seraph blinked in the darkness to make out the face of the man who was giving her pleasure she'd never before experienced, but the room was nearly pitch black, thanks to the thin strip of light coming from under the door as her only light source. Something about him felt familiar, but aside from the shadow of a strong jaw and a dimple, she couldn't identify the perfect stranger.

"Please," she whispered into the darkness, reaching up and running her hands over the man's face, trailing her fingers over the divots that indicated he was smiling down at her before trailing her hands over his shoulders. She was unsure what she was begging for but knew that she needed it desperately.

Strong hands pushed her thighs apart, and the broad shoulders she'd just traced brushed against her most sensitive parts as the man lying between them settled in to worship at her altar. She didn't have to beg—didn't even have time to form a word—because he didn't hesitate, immediately using his stiffened tongue to part her labia and lap in between the folds. He dragged his tongue up and down the length of her slit, tasting every inch of her as she slid her fingers along his smooth scalp and gripped the back of his head, pulling his face even deeper into her pussy, begging him not to stop.

The room might have been dark, but Seraph could see her orgasm shining brightly as if it were a light at the end of a satisfaction tunnel. It was there, just within reach, and the moment she stretched out her hands to grab it, he sucked his tongue back into his mouth and scrambled up her body, laying against her until they were flush against one another with his dick notched between her pussy lips.

"Say my name," he commanded as he rocked his body against hers, dragging the ridged underside of his rock-solid erection along her needy clit. "Say it." Then he grabbed one of her breasts tightly and bent his neck, capturing the stiff nipple with his teeth.

Gasping, she gripped his arms and arched her back off the bed. The added sensation was too much and the pressure… She could feel her climax hurtling toward her. *Just a few more thrusts…*

"Say. It!" he growled, sending a delicious shiver up her spine as she breathed, *"Damon…"*

The shock of speaking those five letters broke through her consciousness, and she jolted awake, heart pounding and breaths heavy. Before she could even begin to process the incredibly erotic—and highly inappropriate—dream she'd awakened from, she realized that a heavy weight had settled over her body and was pressing her into the mattress. It was an almost comforting weight until she recognized the shape of a dick rubbing against her pussy.

Her shoulders tensed as panic seized her. She tried to feel around, but her limbs felt like boulders attached to her body. As she lay there, willing her arms to heed the instructions her brain was commanding, she felt a jolt of sensation between her legs that caused her body to arch off of the bed similarly to the dream she had just abandoned. Her body was buzzing with electricity the same intensity of her subconscious, and when rough hands gripped her waist to anchor her to the bed as he ground against her harder, Seraph's only thoughts were of release.

"Shit!" she cried as the heat that had begun building in her core in her dream intensified and her toes curled.

The numbness in her limbs dissipated, and she quickly wrapped her legs around the mystery god's waist, gripping his biceps tightly as if they were the only thing to keep her from hurtling into space. She'd thought her dream was intense, but this reality was one thousand times better. Lust coated her thoughts, and she was two seconds from begging him to put his dick inside of her when she trailed her hands up his shoulders to his face and mentally stuttered when she came to a familiar jawline. Breaths quickening for an entirely different reason, she let her fingers walk across his skin and nearly screamed when they dipped into two cavernous dimples underlined by a short beard.

This can't be. She had to still be dreaming.

"Da—Damon?"

He grunted absently, obviously focused on what was happening where their bodies met. "Yeah, baby."

As soon as she heard the "y" begin to form in the back of his throat, she started to buck her hips to get him off of her. He'd lost his fucking mind!

"Oh my god, Damon. What the fuck—what are you doing in here?! Get off of me!"

Instead of complying with her command, he used his fingers to dig into her flesh and rotated his hips quickly, successfully shoving her toward her pinnacle.

"Fuuuuck," she moaned, body convulsing as she climaxed beneath him.

He hurriedly lifted off of her and scooted down between her legs, covering her pussy with his mouth. He latched onto her clit with suction so intense that her orgasm ratcheted up several notches and she had to pull the pillow from beneath her head to muffle her screams. A second orgasm quickly ripped through her, and her legs trembled around his head as she begged him to stop, but he was relentless.

"Damon, oh God, please! I can't—I can't..."

However, he ignored her, his palms hot against her thighs as he held them open and devoured her until the pressure became so unbearable that stars burst beneath her eyelids and her eyes rolled into the back of her head. Exhausted, she collapsed against the mattress, her chest heaving, eyes staring unfocused above her until she drifted back to sleep.

A soft knock at the door roused her, and she immediately scrambled to try and cover herself, stopping short when she realized that she was still wearing her silk pajama set. Although she hadn't removed it when she'd first climbed into bed, she distinctly remembered being naked when she woke up with Damon planted between her thighs. Confused, she sat up and pressed the heels of her hands against her eyes. *Had it all been a dream?*

The door opened and Jaime poked her head in the door. "Seraph, you up?"

"Ye—" Seraph coughed to clear the thick, sleep-induced huskiness out of her voice. "Yeah, I'm up. Everything okay?"

The door opened wider, and Jaime stepped into the room.

"Oh!" She stopped short and her eyes widened.

Seraph followed her gaze and sucked in a breath when her eyes landed on Damon, who was lying on his stomach beside her with his arms folded under his head as if he hadn't a care in the world.

"I, uh, I heard a noise—almost like a yell, and I came to see if you were okay."

Nerves gripped Seraph's throat. *Had Jaime heard her moaning Damon's name?*

Laughing lightly, she shook her head and pulled the duvet tighter around her chest. "Oh, my bad. I rolled over in my sleep and this fool scared me. I thought I was going to have a bed to myself."

Squinting, Jaime leaned further into the room, allowing a sliver of light from the hallway to shine on the bed. Seraph prayed that it was still too dark in the room for Jaime to make out Damon's features, but when the other woman's eyes widened and a knowing grin appeared on her face, Seraph realized that her prayer hadn't reached higher than the vaulted ceiling.

"Jaime—"

"Uh, uhn." Jaime shook her head, grinning as wide as her cheeks would stretch. "You don't have to explain anything to me, Miss *I'd Rather Starve Than Choke On Damon's Dick*. I see my passion punch did what it was supposed to do."

Seraph opened her mouth to deny the

assumption, but the look on Jaime's face made her sigh. It would have been a waste of good breath. The other woman backed out of the room until only her head was inside.

"I'll let you get your rest so when the youngin' wakes up for the next round you can be ready." Cackling, Jaime pulled the door closed softly and the light under the door disappeared, casting Seraph in complete darkness with a motionless body beside her. If nothing else, she knew she didn't want to be there when Damon woke up from whatever drug bender he was on.

She didn't think; she just jumped out of the bed and groped along her body to make sure she wasn't in another dream and truly did have on all her clothes, bra included. Satisfied that everything of importance was there, she quietly opened the door and crept out into the hallway, heading for the living room where she knew the basket of keys was. The overhead light was off, but the glow from the muted television bounced off of several faces, in various stages of alertness and slumber. Finding the basket quickly, she dug inside until she found her key fob and immediately slipped out of Jaime's house into the dead of night, determined to forget every salacious memory from that darkened bedroom.

5
LAYING CLAIM

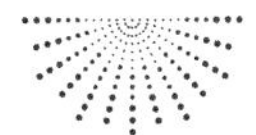

"MAMA? WHERE YOU AT?"

Seraph pushed open the front door of her mother's townhouse and tucked her keys into the pocket of her coat, scanning the open-concept first floor in one swoop. She kicked off her shoes and jogged up the steep flight of steps, checking the two bedrooms and finding them both empty.

"Mama!" She called out once more after she descended the steps and headed to the garage. It was dark and empty, and her mother was nowhere in sight. There was only one last place for her to check. The door that led to the backyard was through the kitchen, so she crisscrossed back through the house from the garage, which was near the front door. As soon as she stepped out onto the porch and looked to her left, she saw her mother leaning against the round glass table, the centerpiece of her patio furniture, holding a glass in her hand. Eyes narrowed, she pursed her lips and pulled the door closed behind her before walking toward her.

"Woman, I have been looking everywhere for you! I need to tell you about—"

The words dried up on her tongue when her mother turned around and Seraph saw who sat at the table. Damon was slouched in the seat opposite Joyce, staring at Seraph with a slight smirk at the corner of his lips and nothing but heat in his eyes. Her gaze flickered from the silent man to her mother, who had set her glass on the table and spread her arms wide.

"Hey, baby! Look who stopped by to see me!" Joyce didn't seem to notice that her daughter had frozen in place with wide eyes trained on the unexpected guest. She crossed the few steps that separated them, wrapping Seraph in a tight hug before kissing her cheek and grabbing her hand to pull her closer to the table. Then she sat down and retrieved her glass that was filled more than halfway with a dark brown liquid that Seraph knew without a doubt was her mother's home-brewed sweet tea.

"I was shredding the chicken for the buffalo macaroni and cheese I was making for our lunch date when the doorbell ring. Imagine my surprise when I saw Damon standing on the other side of the door!" She smiled as Damon pushed his chair back and stood up.

"Where's my hug?" he asked, holding his arms out to Seraph.

Seraph took a step backward and folded her arms across her chest. "What are you doing here, Damon?"

Joyce's smile grew. "Aww, honey, don't be like that. I know our lunches are important to you, but it's okay to have a visitor just this once. Be nice to him." She grabbed Seraph's arm and pushed her directly into the circle of Damon's arms.

Turning at the last moment, Seraph pulled herself up short before colliding with him and tilted at the waist to offer him a side hug. Her aim was to keep as much space in between them as possible, but it didn't seem to matter as Damon pressed his lips to the side of her neck and reached one hand around her back while the other quickly palmed her ass. Gasping, she jerked back, pressing her hands against his chest to push him away.

"Stop, Damon."

"What's going on?" Joyce's sharp voice broke the silence, and Seraph looked over at her mother who stared at the two of them suspiciously. "Are you messing with my baby, Damon?"

Damon shook his head, that irritating smirk still

plastered on his face. "Not at all, Auntie Joyce. Just hugging her too tight."

Lips twisted and eyes narrowed, Seraph turned to her mother. "No, Mama. He grabbed my—"

Before she could finish her sentence, a loud car horn startled her, and her mother's phone immediately began to ring. Seraph watched a pleased look appear on her mother's face as she looked at her phone.

"Hold that thought, baby. My friend is out front." Without giving Seraph an opportunity to ask what she meant by "friend", Joyce took off around the side of the house, fingers running through her sleek bob as she tossed over her shoulder, "You'd better be nice to my baby, Damon, or I'm putting your ass out!"

Not sparing Damon a glance, Seraph immediately bolted back into the house as soon as her mother was out of sight, attempting to put some much-needed distance between the two of them. She rushed into the kitchen, placing her hands on the cool, stone countertop and letting her head hang dejectedly. She'd managed to avoid bumping into Damon at work for the past week and now, he'd shown up at her mother's house? What were the fucking odds? Was he still on drugs? Is that why he felt comfortable gripping her ass in front of her mother as if it was the most natural thing in the world?

"You running from me?"

Shocked, Seraph spun around and locked eyes with Damon, who leaned against the door that led to her mother's backyard. She hadn't heard the ever-present squeal of the screen door opening and closing, and he seemed to appear out of thin air. As she tried to figure out how he had managed to get inside so quietly, the smirk on those full, brown lips of his distracted her. How dare he look at her like that? As if he hadn't just groped her?!

Fueled by her anger, she stalked toward him, cocking her arm back and slapping him across the face.

"Don't you ever again in your life put your hands on my ass, Damon!"

When he didn't so much as blink, she felt a stab of concern slash across her chest and took a single step backward. His lack of reaction was…odd.

He rolled his head in a circle, cracking his neck in the process before meeting her gaze again. The smirk had finally dropped from his face.

"Can I put my mouth on it?"

"You're a—huh?"

"What about my dick?" He stepped toward her, and she answered his movement by taking another step back.

Damon dragged his tongue along his bottom lip.

"You told me not to put my hands on your ass again, so I asked if I could use my mouth or my dick instead." He continued forward until Seraph's back hit the counter. He placed one hand on the counter behind her and the other on her waist, the heat from his fingers singeing her over the thin fabric of her dress.

"What about… in it?" he asked in a low, sensual voice. "Can I put my dick in your ass, Seraph?"

She swallowed over the lump in her throat and stared up into the eyes of the man she'd known since he was six years old. There was nothing recognizable in those brown depths, and that was perhaps more terrifying than the way her body heated at his lewd questions.

"Damon, what the hell are you doing?!" Her voice was barely higher than a whisper, the words straining to jump out of her mouth.

"Isn't it obvious?" he asked with a single brow raised. "I'm being nice to Auntie Joyce's baby."

Seraph's eyes were wide, her mouth hanging open for a moment before she snapped it shut and shook her head, lifting her arms between them to frame his face with her hands. "Are you on drugs? Is that it? You can tell me, and I'll help you find some resources. I won't even tell Uncle Louis, I swear. Just tell me what's going on with you." Her voice had taken on a desperate note that she didn't even try to hide. His actions had her so confused; she didn't know how to categorize them. *What was going on here?*

"If it was drugs, would they make *you* feel good, Ser, because that's all I want to do. I want to make you feel good so that you scream my name like you did at that party. Can I do that?"

Slowly, Seraph shook her head. His eyes had darkened from a warm brown to something akin to mud after it rained, and everything inside of Seraph was telling her to run as quickly and as far away as she could. But she didn't get the chance because faster than she could process his already brazen behavior, Damon's hand slid off of her waist and slipped underneath her skirt to rest on her panty-covered mound. His mouth dropped to her neck, and he kissed her softly before speaking directly into her ear.

"Are you sure?

Sliding his palm against her, he used his middle finger to rub along her slit, soaking the crotch of her panties in her juices.

Sucking in a breath, she grabbed his wrist. "Don't do this."

"Why?" he murmured, licking the shell of her ear.

She whimpered, her fingers tightening around his wrist. "Because… it's wrong."

Biting her earlobe, he growled. "When has an orgasm ever been wrong?" Then he pulled her panties to the side and slid a finger into her opening.

"Oh my God," she cried out softly as her hips bucked of their own volition.

He slid a second finger into her and began pumping quickly. Heat engulfed her belly, and the way she widened her stance was an unconscious reaction, her head falling back against her shoulders as she panted heavily. When Damon leaned forward and nipped at her throat with his teeth, he added a third finger, and she shuddered at the intrusion—at how full she felt.

"What's my name?" he asked.

Eyes closed, she shook her head, refusing to answer him.

His thumb dug into her folds until it found her clit, and her eyes popped open to find him staring at her intensely. "Answer me," he demanded.

Her mouth parted as her bottom lip curled in and tucked under her teeth. His eyes narrowed at her defiance, prompting him to pump into her faster until her knees weakened and her toes curled in her flats. She gripped his forearms as her climax sped toward her like a bullet train.

"Shit! Damon!" she hissed. "*Fuuuuck*!"

She slumped against him, moaning when he pulled his fingers from inside her, the wet sound echoing in the quiet kitchen. He sucked the three digits into his mouth, and as she watched him clean her juices from his hand, the reality of what just happened hit her harder than her orgasm had.

Not again! she thought, her face pinching into a frown. Before Damon could say another word, she ducked under the arm he still had anchored on the counter behind her and sprinted toward the front door. With trembling fingers, she pulled her keys from her pocket and jogged toward her car. Her mother was standing in the street, grinning up into the face of some man that Seraph didn't recognize, but she was too flustered to do anything about it. She eased her car out of the driveway and rolled down the window to call out a goodbye to Joyce before speeding off down the street and navigating out of the neighborhood.

She couldn't blame this one on sleep, and it didn't seem like she could blame it on drugs either. He hadn't been bleary-eyed nor had slurred speech, and when she thought about it, neither of those symptoms had been present the night of Jaime's party. Maybe the truth was that Damon had a side of him that no one ever saw—a side that she would have never believed existed. Where he had always seemed shy and reserved, he was now full of bravado and perversion, and for some reason had fixated on her. Her thoughts went from wondering what was wrong with him to figuring out how to avoid him at all costs.

There was no way she was letting him put his hands, mouth, or any other body part near her again.

6
EXPLAIN YOURSELF

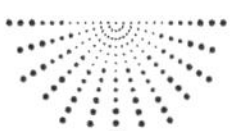

"HEIFER, I KNOW YOU DIDN'T LEAVE WITHOUT SAYING anything?!"

Seraph sighed as her mother screeched into her ear and lifted her shoulder to hold her phone to her face as she unlocked the door of her apartment. She'd been anticipating this call and was surprised it had taken an hour to come. Those sixty minutes had given her enough time to browse the aisles at *Poured* in search of the perfect bottle of sweet wine to drown her woes in tonight.

Walking inside, she locked the door behind her and disengaged the alarm before dropping her keys onto an end table and kicking out of her shoes as she made her way to the kitchen.

"I said bye, Mama."

Joyce sucked her teeth, and Seraph dug her trusty

rabbit wine bottle opener out of a drawer and fixed it to the top of the wine.

"No. What you did was yell out some mess from the front seat of your car *as* you were driving off! That's not the same thing at all. You weren't even here ten minutes. You didn't even get to eat!"

"I know, I know! I'm sorry. I'm just having a crisis right now and prefer to be alone."

As soon as Seraph heard Joyce's sharp intake of breath, she silently cursed herself for her poor choice of words.

"A…crisis? What's going on?"

The good-natured fussing in her tone had been replaced by stern concern, and Seraph rushed to reassure her.

"It's not a crisis, Mama. That's not the right word. I'm…dealing with a situation that I need to work through. It's *not* a crisis," she reiterated, "but there is a moral aspect that I need to figure out."

"Moral?" Joyce asked, confusion radiating through the phone lines. "Did you commit a crime?"

Seraph dropped the rabbit opener onto the counter and carried the now-open bottle of wine with her into her bedroom.

"No, Mama. I did not commit a crime."

"You sleeping with your boss?"

Chuckling, she put the phone on speaker and

placed it on her nightstand as she began removing her jewelry and putting it in the velvet-lined box on her dresser.

"As much as I adore Gina, no, ma'am. I'm not sleeping with her."

"You rob somebody?"

"Well," Seraph began wryly, "since robbing someone is definitely a crime, I'm going to have to say no, ma'am."

"Did you—"

"Mama, come on!"

Joyce's laughter brought a smile to Seraph's face, even as she rolled her eyes.

"Well, shit. If you won't tell me, I have to guess."

Seraph grabbed her phone and carried it with her into her closet as she disrobed.

"I'm not ready to tell you just yet. I thought I was but…I just need you to exercise a little patience. Remember how you used to tell me it was a virtue when I was growing up? Well, I need you to remember that right now."

"Seraph Soleil."

At the use of her first and middle names, Seraph groaned. "Yes, ma'am?"

"You know you can talk to me about anything, right?"

"Yes, ma'am. I know." It was something Joyce had

said to her dozens of times during her childhood and well into her teenage years. Having come from a home where freedom of expression was a punishable offense, Joyce made sure that her daughter never felt as if she had to censor herself.

"And even though I can't promise I'll understand, I can promise not to judge you too harshly or put undue pressure on you."

The earnestness in her mother's voice made a lump form in Seraph's throat. "I know, Mama. I love you."

"I love you more, baby. Never forget that. Now, I'll let you go. I can hear an echo, so I'm assuming you're in your bathroom."

Seraph nodded, even though the other woman couldn't see her. "Yes, ma'am. I'll call you tomorrow."

"You'd better."

Then the call disconnected and Seraph sat her phone on the counter while she started the water for her shower. She needed to clean away all evidence of what Damon had done to her then she planned to climb into her bed and binge on some feel-good shows and put all thoughts of him out of her head.

7
BANG MY LINE

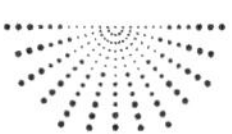

HER PHONE RANG FOUR TIMES IN A ROW BEFORE SHE silenced the ringer and put the damned thing in the drawer of her nightstand. Damon had been calling her nonstop for the past hour, and she was one more call away from blocking his number. He didn't leave messages. He didn't text. He just hung up and redialed.

He was wasting his time because Seraph did not intend to answer for him. There was nothing for them to discuss. Sure, she had a handful of questions to ask him about the things he'd done to her and the reasons that fueled him, but after their encounter earlier that day, she didn't think she could be in a room alone with him long enough to get the answers she needed.

A peculiar, rhythmic knocking on her door pulled

her attention from the show she was watching on her tablet. Exhaling an annoyed breath, she stared at the wall in front of her that separated her bedroom from the rest of her 800-square foot apartment and contemplated whether or not to go answer the door. It was after nine, and not only was she already in bed, but she'd set the security alarm in anticipation of not leaving her bedroom until daybreak. None of her friends would show up this late without calling first, and her mother had both a key and the code to her alarm.

Her brows furrowed and she frowned when the knocking sounded once more, trying to think of who it could be without her taking the easy route and simply checking. Then, a light bulb clicked on in her head, and she shot up from her prone position as it occurred to her who was likely at her door.

Damon.

It *had* to be him. She lacked the words to explain how she knew, but her surety was undeniable. Also undeniable was the unwanted but intense heat curling in her belly at the memory of being filled by Damon's fingers. That was enough to make her lie back down and pull the covers up over her head.

The last thing she needed was Damon in her apartment. Letting him in would be playing a dangerous game, one she wasn't sure wouldn't end with her face down, ass up, and her brain muddled with confusion and shame.

When the knocking continued, her eyes darted to her nightstand and she quickly played a round of heads or tails in her head to help her decide whom she should call—her complex's security or the police. Just as the mental coin landed with heads up, her work phone began to chime. The initially low ringtone ascended with each run until she was certain whoever stood on her porch could hear it without straining. Throwing back the covers, she leaped out of bed and rushed into the living room where her work phone was charging on one of the two end tables that bookended her small couch. After silencing the device, she sighed loudly and stared at the front door, willing her solicitor to change their mind and go away.

As soon as that thought crossed her mind, the knock sounded again. Groaning, Seraph flicked on a lamp and stomped over to the door to punch in the four-digit code and disengage her security alarm. Pushing up onto her tiptoes, she looked through the peephole, cursing softly when all she saw was blackness. Whoever was at her door had covered the tiny window with their finger. For some reason, that small action only seemed to cement Seraph's thought that it was indeed Damon. Taking a deep breath, she threw back the deadbolt and eased the door inward a few inches. Instead of standing in the opening, she used the door as a shield, keeping most of her body hidden from the person who stood on the other side. With wide eyes, she took him in. It was the same man who had finger-fucked her into an orgasm in her mother's kitchen just ten hours earlier.

He was also the man who'd, as a kindergartner, come into her life when she was fifteen and her uncle married his mother. The man that she'd babysat off and on until she was eighteen. The man who had taken the boundaries of their relationship and burned them to the ground, turning the box she'd kept him in on its head. This was the man who, out of nowhere, seemed determined to tie her mind—and body—in knots.

His dark brown skin seemed to glisten under her porch light as he stared down at her with an impassive look on his face. Stretched across his chest was a plain white t-shirt that clung to his pectorals and was partially visible under a half-zipped university hoodie. A pair of sweatpants clung to his waist and thighs, displaying an obvious erection that her eyes stuttered over and gave her pause. Involuntarily, her mind transported her to Jaime's party and the memory of him rubbing against her bare sex. Her brain screamed at her to look away from his dick, but she just couldn't peel her eyes away from it.

She was literally dickmatized.

By her cousin.

The thought made guilt dance in the back of her brain, but the thumping between her thighs, the steady pulse that felt as if her pussy had a heartbeat of its own, worked that guilt into the shadows.

Hell was her destination and her transportation was soaked in gasoline. Unleaded. Ninety-three octanes.

"Damon," she began, shaking her head slowly and willing—begging—her body to calm down enough to send him away, "what are you doing here?"

A moment of silence passed between them before he leaned against the partially opened doorframe. "Why didn't you answer the phone when I called you?"

Finally, she jerked her gaze up to his face to see his lips twisted into a knowing smirk that instantly irritated her. Obviously, he knew what she was looking at, and his amusement made shame bite at her cheeks.

Her knuckles whitened as she clenched the door and gritted out, "Which time?"

He lifted one dark eyebrow at the infusion of attitude in her voice. "The last time."

She huffed, blowing air out of her nose. "I was tired of you calling me."

He nodded as if it made perfect sense to him. "And the first time?"

Rolling her eyes, she shot back, "I didn't want to talk to you."

He stared at her so long that she began to fidget, and she was too damn old to be fidgeting under anyone's stare. Her neck heated with anger and embarrassment, and just as she opened her mouth to tell him to go away, he spoke.

"That's fine. We don't *have* to talk."

The implication in his words was as clear as glass, and her breathing grew shallow as anticipation settled into her belly. She blinked rapidly at her internal reaction to his words, and a tendril of panic snaked its way up her throat.

"Look, Damon—"

"Let me see you," he said, and although he spoke softly, the demand was clearly understood.

Despite wanting to slam the door in his face and run back to bed, Seraph felt a buzzing in her ears that compelled her to do the opposite. Like a marionette attached to an invisible string, Seraph pulled the door open wider and shuffled into the doorway. She stood frozen in place as Damon's eyes traveled from her sock-covered feet, up her bare thighs where the hem of her sleeping gown began, then paused where the juncture of her thighs rested under her gown before skirting up her torso to her face.

The hunger in his eyes caused a gush of moisture to ruin her panties and gooseflesh to bubble all over her body. Was it possible to be aroused and terrified at the same damn time?

When Damon reached down and squeezed his dick over his sweats, Seraph clenched her thighs together and took a step backward, hand gripping the doorknob tightly. Her mind screamed for her to close and lock the door—to put some distance in between the two of them until he came to his senses, no matter how long that took—but that same compulsion that pulled her from behind the door rooted her where she stood, making her wait for his next move.

Silently, Damon stepped over the threshold of her apartment, removing her hand from the knob and pushing the door closed behind him. She walked backward, stumbling over her own feet as she tried not to get run over by his commanding presence. He reached out, wrapping his fingers around her wrist and pulling her flush against his body.

"Careful," he said, his tone laced with a warning

that she wasn't sure how to process. Did he mean that she should be careful with her steps or careful with how she handled him? She couldn't figure it out and refused to ask because the last thing she needed was any sort of clarification about *anything* from him. All she needed was for him to exit her apartment and —maybe—move back to Dallas.

Pulling out of his grasp, she backed up until she could step around one of the armchairs in her living room, putting some much-needed space in between them.

"It's late and I need to go to bed."

He shoved his hands into his pockets, his eyes trained on her. "You're right."

She sighed, her shoulders drooping with relief. "Thank you."

With quick strides, she crossed the living room, her hand outstretched as she reached for the doorknob. And just as her hand made contact with the cool metal, she felt the heat of Damon's body against her back as his hands fell to her hips, freezing her in place. His lips grazed her neck, and the soft touch made each of the tiny hairs all over her body stand on end as a full-body shiver consumed her. She bit her lip to stifle the soft moan that tried to escape from her mouth. He didn't need to be encouraged by her.

Determined fingers trailed down her thighs until they reached the hem of her gown. He bunched the fabric into his fists and slowly lifted it up her body.

Swallowing against the lump in her throat, Seraph curved her hips forward, trying to move them away from the hard body standing behind her.

"Da—think about this, don't—"

He released the fabric and slid his hands underneath, sliding his palms up her torso until he reached her unrestrained breasts. Cupping each globe in his hands, he rubbed his nose along the shell of her ear.

"Don't… stop?" He pinched and pulled at her nipples, and her head fell forward, hitting the door with a thud as she tried to bite back a moan, succeeding only in forcing out the sound from the back of her throat. "Okay." He wrapped an arm under her breasts and used his knee to nudge her legs apart. For all her protesting, her legs spread easily, and he stuck two fingers in his mouth before shoving them inside of her panties and expertly finding her clit, massaging it intently with the wet digits.

"Come for me," he murmured against her ear once she began grinding against his hand. "I need it."

He rubbed her until she was squirming in his arms and then dropped to his knees, pulling down her panties as he descended and pushing her legs as wide as they could go with her underwear as a restraint. He attacked her clit from behind, the different angle adding another level of sensation that made Seraph press her hot cheek against the cool door.

"When are you going to stop pretending you don't want this?"

"I'm...*ooh*...not pretending," she murmured breathlessly, fighting not to close her legs while succumbing to the climax that was determined to take her under. "I don't want this. I *don't* want you. *I can't.*"

"That's too bad." Damon's voice was an even cadence that belied the havoc he was wreaking on her. "He sure as fuck wants you."

She panted. "Huh? What do you—I'm—this is *wrong*. Ah!" A shockwave rocked her and her body began to quake. "Soooo wrong," she moaned.

Licking a trail from the cuff of her ass cheek to the base of her spine, Damon slipped his thumb into her contracting folds and asked, "But how does it feel?"

Her response was lost as her orgasm crested. She shot up on her tiptoes and cried out as she shook uncontrollably, gripping the doorknob to keep herself grounded. When her heels touched the floor, Damon stood and spun her around.

"I'm going to fuck you. Right now."

Chest heaving and pussy grasping at air, trying like hell to latch on to something, Seraph tried one more tactic to derail this train.

"What would your father say if he heard you say that to me?" Surely, her Uncle Louis would grab Damon by the scruff of his neck and shake some sense into him.

Instead of answering, Damon dragged her across the room and pushed her face down on the couch with her ass hiked in the air.

"I told Louis how much I want you, how badly I needed you, and you know what he said to me?" He pulled her panties completely off, tossing the constricting material dismissively.

"What did he say?" She turned her head to watch as he then tugged his shirt over his head and pushed his pants down. A whimper oozed from her mouth as she took in his immaculate dick and the gorgeous body it was attached to. Those shoulders and the sprinkling of kinky hair across his chest; the steely, dark-brown rod jutting out from his hips. She swallowed hard and felt the muscles in her pussy clench in anticipation.

"He said 'If she's anything like her mother, it'll be the best pussy you've ever had'."

He licked his hand and pumped his dick once,

twice, before climbing onto the couch behind her and lifting one of her legs to rest on the back of the couch.

Shocked and disgusted by his response, but incredibly turned on by everything he'd already done to her, she gasped and closed her eyes. "I don't believe you."

"That's too bad," he said once more. "You know what I need, Seraph. Give it to me."

"What about what I need?" The question came out in a puff of air, and she moaned as he rubbed the head of his dick up and down her slit, coating it with her juices.

"And what is it that you need, Seraph, besides this dick inside of you as soon as possible?"

"I—" She swallowed her misgivings. At this point, it was obvious what was about to happen, so fighting it was moot. "I need you to fuck me until I come so hard that I get cross-eyed. Fuck me until I grow hoarse from screaming. Give it to me so good that I'm walking with a limp tomorrow. This is completely insane and can only happen once, so I want you to make it count. Can you do that?"

Rubbing a hand along her hips, butt, and thighs, making her shudder under his touch, he sank into her in one, smooth motion. Seraph shook her head, smushing her face into the seat cushions, not understanding how he could feel *so good* when everything about this was as wrong as two left shoes. Her back arched and it took a moment for her to catch her breath as he held still once he was as deep as he could go. *Had she ever in her life felt as full as she did right this moment?*

Damon chuckled and the huskiness of his voice caused another full-body shake to run through her. "Only once, huh? Well, I can give you all of that and more…if you let me."

Then, he gripped her hips and started fucking her as if she'd unleashed a beast that had something to prove. He pistoned in and out of her, employing a stroke too fast for her to think straight, let alone breathe evenly. With her leg hiked up, every stroke of his dick hit a spot inside of her that had her eyes rolling to the back of her head and inaudible gurgles spewing from her lips.

"Do you know how good this pussy is?" Damon grunted, his fingers digging into her fleshy waist as he pulled her back against him, again and again, with each thrust, the lewd sound of their skin smacking together in her living room an erotic soundtrack to their movements. "So fucking amazing," he groaned. "*Shit.* No wonder he was obsessed with you."

Gasping after a particularly hard thrust, Seraph asked, "Who…ah…was obsessed…*oh*…with me?"

Instead of responding, Damon dipped his fingers

in the creamy wet mess she'd made on his dick and reached around, finding her clit with his deft fingers. As he thrust back and forth, he circled the nub repeatedly until Seraph's body tightened and she came all over his dick in a wet gush.

"Shiiiiiit!" she cried, her hips jerking of their own accord as her core tightened around him.

He didn't give her much time to come down before he pulled out of her and grabbed her arm, attempting to make her stand up. When he let her go, her knees wobbled for a moment, and she dropped back down to the couch. Squatting in front of her, he ignored the dazed look on her face as she stared at his still-hard dick. He grabbed her chin and tilted her head up until he could get a clear look at her eyes, smirking in the process.

"Hmm. Not cross-eyed yet, I see. Let's go."

Seraph sucked in a breath as he lifted her into his arms and started down the hallway. She directed him to her bedroom where he deposited her on the bed before pushing her back and crawling in between her thighs until he was face-to-face with her glistening, swollen folds. He gave her a quick glance, and the gleam in his eye shortened her breath.

What in the hell had she agreed to?

8

WORK HUSBAND

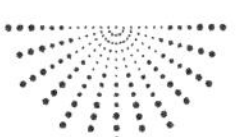

It hadn't taken Seraph very long to understand why Damon had chuckled after she'd told him they could only have sex once. He didn't leave her apartment until he had wrested every orgasm he could from her and she lay boneless and unconscious across her bed. When she finally awoke the next day, it was early afternoon, and she was pleased to be deliciously sore and still a bit unstable on her legs. If she was going to backstroke her way into some sin, at least it had been worth it.

Thankfully, it was a Sunday, and she was able to soak in the tub with some Epsom salts before calling to schedule a last-minute massage at *Kneaded* with her favorite therapist. Luckily, Shana's evening appointment had canceled and she was able to take

Seraph for a seventy-five-minute session instead of their usual fifty.

The next day, she bounced into work in a good mood, smiling and waving, as she passed through the lobby to get to the elevators. The people inside held the door for her and even complimented her on her hair. Her twists were still holding despite the way Damon had wrapped them around his hand as he fucked her from the back two days prior.

Gina—her boss for seven of the last twelve years she'd been with the company—stopped by to congratulate her on a terrific quarter, and when the mail cart came around, there was nothing for her. The day was progressing splendidly. Seraph had kicked off her shoes and was singing along to the soft music playing on her phone as she worked through her emails when the door to her office opened suddenly. Startled, she clutched at her chest, her eyes widening in surprise, as Damon entered the room and closed the door behind him. She didn't miss how he locked the door, and the action made her stomach clench. Her eyes flew to his face.

"What are you doing here?"

Walking toward her, he started rolling up the sleeves of his shirt. "It's lunchtime."

Glancing at the clock in the bottom right corner of her computer monitor, Seraph noted that it was just after noon. It had been a couple of weeks since they'd gone to lunch together, but in light of recent developments, she thought it best to forgo them for a while.

"I can't get away right now. These emails are calling my name, and I can't ignore that for even an hour. Besides, we should probably chill on the—" Damon had rounded her desk and rolled her seat back, putting a stop to her words immediately. Heart thumping, she gripped the arms of her chair.

"Damon, what the hell are you doing?!"

He eyed her and tossed his tie over his shoulder. "I already told you."

She was shaking her head before he could even finish the sentence. Nah. He couldn't be implying what it sounded like.

Except...apparently, he was.

He pulled her out of her chair and spun her around to face her desk then tugged at the leg of her slacks until the elastic waistband slid down her hips and the material gathered at her knees. Hand at her back, he ignored her continued questions and pushed her forward until her chest rested on the desk. Next, he sat in the chair he'd just removed her from and spread her cheeks with his hands before diving, tongue first, into her pussy.

He licked and slurped noisily, seemingly

unconcerned that it was the middle of the day and they were in a very crowded office building with only one door separating them from the rest of Seraph's department. Seraph stretched her arms on either side of her and gripped the edges of her glass desk as she held on for dear life while he feasted on her flesh. When he added his fingers to the party, slipping and sliding through her folds before finding her clit between her still clenched thighs, her body began to quake. She jerked in his hold, reflexively trying to run from the sensations he was commanding from inside of her.

"Why now?" she managed to ask, grunting the words out as the desk bit into her stomach. There was more to the question, but her voice failed her. *Why at this moment? Why at work? Why in her office? Why?*

He pulled his tongue from inside of her, and she wasn't sure if she was angrier at him for stopping or herself for asking a question that required his mouth to answer.

"I can't even think straight if my face isn't between your legs. Don't deny me this."

His words triggered something inside of her, and before she knew it, she was coming. Heat flooded her body, and the stiff points of her nipples pressed into the desk as her orgasm washed over her. She panted and gasped and whisper-shouted curses, working overtime to keep her voice from being heard on the other side of the door that just wasn't built to contain these kinds of sounds. As the waves subsided, she released the edges of the desk and slid her palms against the top, thinking she was about to get up, but the head of Damon's dick at her entrance made her moan and collapse back into position.

"*Damon,*" she whined, "I thought we said we'd only do this once."

He pushed inside of her, chunks of her ass clenched between each of his palms. He groaned and landed a sharp slap to one of her cheeks. "I never said that shit. That was all you."

"It's…*shit*…the right thing to do."

She felt several of her twists lift from her shoulders as Damon wrapped them around his fist like boxer's tape. "The right thing for you to do is to take this dick."

He didn't really leave her any choice as he pulled her hair with one hand and squeezed her ass with the other as he began thrusting into her without preamble. Her eyes fluttered closed as she succumbed to his instruction. With her chest rising off of the desk and her neck bent backward, she rolled her hips in time with his thrusts, trying to give as good as she was getting.

A rough chuckle alerted her that Damon figured out what she was doing. Instead of responding, he wrapped an arm around her waist, and suddenly, she felt the disarming sensation of falling before she landed in his lap, still connected to him, and realized that he had sat down in her chair.

"You wanted to work," he husked, "so work."

No additional were needed. Seraph gripped the arms of her chair and wound her hips over him, grinding in his lap so that every rotation made the head of his dick scrape against a spot inside of her that her had hissing and moaning above him. With her in the driver's seat, solely focused on her own release, it didn't take long for that familiar feeling to rise up her body again. She trembled as another orgasm surged toward her, her movements becoming jerky and uncoordinated.

"Yeah," Damon murmured appreciatively as his hand trailed up her body, under her blouse, until he was cupping her breasts over her bra. "Give me that nut. I fucking need that shit." He thumbed her hardened nipples through the thin material, and her head fell back against his shoulder, the added effect too much for her to handle. Biting her lip, she stilled in his lap and groaned as she came once again.

He lifted her off his dick and pushed her chest back onto the desk, and before Seraph had a moment to anticipate his next move, she felt several splashes of hot come land on her bare ass. Without moving from her position on the desk, she flailed her hand around until she reached the top drawer on her desk and pulled it open. She rummaged around until her fingers closed over a package of tissues, but as she tried to awkwardly bend her arm and pull it toward her, it was plucked out of her hand. The sound of the perforation being broken open was loud in the quiet room. She held her breath as Damon wiped all traces of his spend from her skin before gasping when his tongue touched the curve of her cheek in an open-mouthed kiss. He tugged her slacks and underwear back up and stood back when she straightened and turned to face him.

Grabbing her chin, he tilted her head up until they were eye-to-eye. "Next time, I'mma feed it to you."

Her eyes closed and she shuddered at the promise in his voice. His hand fell from her face, and when she opened her eyes, he was opening the door and walking out. Leaning against her desk, she readjusted her panties and slacks and made sure her boobs weren't hanging out of her bra.

Not even two minutes after Damon walked out of her office there was a sharp knock on her door. She hurried back across the room, swiping at her pant legs, praying there were no stains on them and pulled open the door to reveal Vanessa and Sierra standing there with twin grins on their faces. She hadn't been expecting them, but it wasn't unusual for the two of them to pop up on her and pull her away from her computer for a long lunch. Twyla didn't have the freedom to join in, and it was something she always pouted about when they discussed it later. Stepping aside, Seraph let her friends inside her office and self-consciously tugged at the hem of her blouse while their backs were to her.

"Was that Damon we just saw leaving your office?"

"Oh? Yeah, probably. He stopped by to invite me to lunch, but I have too much work to do."

Sierra eyed her shrewdly. "Mmmhm. That's weird because he was adjusting his tie and buttoning his cufflinks. Did he take all of that off to ask you to lunch?"

"Mmhmm," Vanessa cosigned.

Reaching up, Seraph tugged the loose elastic out of her twists and fixed her ruined ponytail. "He was probably fixing that stuff because it was a mess after the afternoon delight he'd had."

Vanessa's mouth dropped open, and Sierra jumped out of her chair.

"Afternoon delight?? Bitch, are you saying what I think you're saying?"

Folding her arms across her chest, Vanessa smirked. "It sounds like she's saying she just gave Damon some pussy for lunch."

Seraph covered her face with her hands and shook her head as she laughed. "He definitely ate, so I guess you would be right, Nessa."

Both women squealed, and Seraph rolled her eyes playfully. She hadn't known how they would react to the news, but she had planned to err on the side of caution and withhold all information until she had forgotten the memory of Damon's dick inside of her. With her plans promptly ruined, she had to say that she was relieved that things seemed to be okay so far.

"How long has this been going on, and why are we just finding out?!"

"It's not like that, Nessa. This is technically the second time. The first was on Saturday. I haven't been holding out on y'all."

"Saturday! The second time?!" Sierra's exclamation was punctuated by her fanning herself comically.

"And at work too," Vanessa added. "So scandalous!"

Seraph rolled her eyes to the ceiling as she chuckled. "I'm still wrapping my mind around the fact that I've fucked Damon; I haven't even processed the office sex yet."

Vanessa shrugged. "As soon as Damon came back from Dallas, looking grown-man-fine and eying you like the last biscuit on the plate, I knew you two motherfuckers would be kissin' cousins one day."

Seraph shrieked with laughter and covered her face again. "Welp," she said through the gaps in her fingers, "just put a bottle of moonshine in my hand and call me a hillbilly."

"Nah," Vanessa countered. "I'll put a crown on you and call you a royal. They're the ones regularly fucking their cousins, all in the name of purity of race or some inane shit."

They all laughed and Seraph swept her eyes back and forth between her two friends. They may have joked about her being with Damon once every blue moon, but their lack of…disgust was really throwing her for a loop.

"Y'all are seriously okay with this?"

Sierra looked at Vanessa then they both looked at Seraph and nodded. "I mean…everybody's grown. Shit, that nigga is almost thirty. Why *wouldn't* we be?"

Sitting back in her chair, Seraph huffed out a sigh. "All jokes aside, for the obvious reasons. I mean…I was fully expecting someone to call me a nasty bitch."

Face pinched in disgust, Sierra rolled her eyes. "You *are* a nasty bitch, but not because you're getting your back broke by your uncle's stepson. You're a nasty bitch because you're standing in a puddle of jizz."

Eyes wide, Seraph looked down between her legs, and sure enough, the toe of her right shoe was sitting in a small puddle of what was undoubtedly Damon's semen.

"Holy shit!" She yanked open the same drawer of her desk that held the tissues and pulled out a package of antibacterial wipes, leaning down to mop up the stain. "I can't believe this," she muttered to herself.

Sierra sucked her teeth. "I can't believe you didn't swallow. I'm so disappointed in you. I know for a fact that I taught you better than this."

Sputtering with laughter, Seraph looked at her friend and shook her head. "You're a damn nut, you know that?"

9
FAMILY MATTERS

"IT WAS GOOD OF YOU TO HELP DAMON GET ON WITH your company. Louis said that he'd been having a hard time finding something in his field after the startup he was working for collapsed. Said he came home from Dallas with his tail between his legs. You might've saved his life."

Seraph's eyes bucked. The very last thing she wanted to talk about was Damon. She was at her mother's house for their weekly shared meal that Damon—thankfully—hadn't crashed again after that first time.

Not after he got what he wanted from her. Was *still* getting what he wanted.

"Mama, all I did was mention his name to the department head. You're acting like I hired him myself."

Smacking her lips, Joyce pinned her daughter with a firm stare. "No, I'm giving credit where credit is due. *You* told him to apply for the position, and *you* made sure that the hiring manager would be looking for his name. *You* got him the job, Seraph."

Eyes on her plate as she sliced into her pecan-crusted chicken breast, Seraph shook her head. Yeah, she'd done all of that before she'd known how he really was. If she could go back in time, she would have kept her mouth shut. "His education and experience got him the job.

Joyce pursed her lips. "He never would have known about it if you hadn't called him, and *those* words came *straight* from Damon's mouth, thank you very much. So, all this modesty is unnecessary." She waved her hand as if fanning away Seraph's words.

Mentally rolling her eyes—because although she was thirty-six, she still wasn't bold enough to do it in her mother's face—Seraph sighed. "Okay, Mama. I hear you."

With a satisfied harrumph, Joyce returned to her food, and Seraph did the same. They fell into a comfortable silence as they enjoyed the meal Joyce had prepared. After a few moments, Joyce looked up with a gleam in her eye.

"You know," she started, wiping her mouth with

her napkin, "helping Damon out like this is only going to make his little crush on you worse."

Brows lifted, Seraph's heart beat a little faster as she asked, "What you mean, Mama? Damon doesn't have a crush on me."

Joyce smirked. "Yes he does, and everybody knows it. That boy has been in love with you since he was twelve-years-old, and apparently, it never went away."

Seraph frowned and forked the last bite of her chicken into her mouth. She needed to find an emergency exit for this conversation. Whatever love her mother thought Damon felt for her was nonexistent as far she knew. What she did know was that *love* had absolutely nothing to do with what was between them. It was a numbers game; how many times could Damon make her come a day. She somehow both lost and won each and every time.

"Well, if that's true, it's disgusting because when he was twelve, I was twenty-one." Chewing, she shrugged. "But I'm sure it's not true, so it doesn't matter."

Joyce observed her quietly for a moment before a shrewd smirk came across her face. "Girl, I said that boy has a crush on you, and you're acting like I said you're in love with him. For all of your denying of his emotions, you're making me think you must like him too." She sat forward in her seat. "Do you?"

Slapping her hands on the table, Seraph sat back in her chair. "Are we in the twilight zone? Did you forget that Damon is *family*? He's your nephew. My cousin. When did you become okay with incest? Who else in the family is it okay for me to be with, huh? Tell me, Mama!"

Joyce made a loud, clucking sound, and Seraph grinned, glad to give the older woman a little of her own frustrating medicine. "Girl, don't play with me. That boy ain't no kin of yours."

Cocking her head to the side, Seraph blinked owlishly at her mother. "Since when? If Damon isn't my cousin, then why do I call his daddy *Uncle* Louis? Why does he call you *Auntie* Joyce? Riddle me that, Mama."

"Don't get smart with me, heifer. Louis is your daddy's brother, and you know good and well that Louis married that boy's mama when he was in elementary school. *That's* why you call him Uncle Louis, but there is no blood relation between you and Damon."

Seraph scoffed. "Blood isn't the only thing that makes people family. You know that better than anyone with all of the men who came into our lives and called themselves my uncle after my daddy died.

You gained a lot of brothers back then, or did you forget?" She quirked an eyebrow at her mother, certain that she had bested her.

With that selfsame smirk returning to her face, Joyce sat back in her chair and shook her head before meeting her daughter's gaze. "I would have thought you'd figured it out by now, baby."

"Figured out what?"

Joyce giggled as if Seraph had told a joke instead of asked a valid question. "Seraph, I was fucking every man that called himself your uncle."

A strangled sound erupted from Seraph's mouth and her eyes ballooned.

"Mama, NO!"

Her giggle morphing into a full-on laugh, Joyce nodded. "Oh, *yes*."

Seraph blinked rapidly as she suddenly remembered something Damon had said to her the first time they'd had sex at her apartment. She'd been adamant then that he was lying, but now that she sat across from her cackling mother, she wondered if maybe she'd just been *hoping* that he was lying. She cringed, already anticipating the answer to her next question.

"Not...*all* of my uncles, right?"

Throwing her head back, Joyce's laugh seemed to grow in volume. Her shoulders shook and wiped a few tears from her eyes. Seraph sat there, her face scrunched into a pout as she waited for her mother to answer her. Finally, Joyce lowered her head and winked, looking so damn tickled that Seraph couldn't stand it.

"I said 'every man' right?"

"Oh my God."

"Mmhmm. Now tell me again about your *family*."

With her argument coming to bite her in the butt, Seraph quickly shifted her focus.

"Okay, okay. Relation aside, Mama please; he's a child, which is why I don't believe this mess you're saying in the first place. If he had a crush on anyone, it would be with someone his own age. Now, can I just eat my food in peace? Please?"

Grinning like the Cheshire cat that caught the cream, Joyce dropped her fork onto her plate and clapped her hands. "Ooh! You *do* like him don't you?"

Seraph pressed her face into her hands and groaned loudly. She'd expected a nice meal with her mother, completely free from the man who was taking up residence in her mind and her bed. The jokes from her friends were funny because that's all they were: jokes. But this? Her mother may have been smiling, but she wouldn't say some off-the-wall stuff like this unless she genuinely didn't have a problem with it. What was in the damn water lately?

"You're killing me, Mama."

Joyce held up her hands. "Okay, okay. I'll leave it alone. All I was trying to say is that if we lived in a state that required blood testing before they issued a marriage license, you and Damon would have no problem obtaining one. Because you aren't blood relatives. That's all. I won't say anything else."

"You've already said enough," Seraph mumbled under her breath. Grabbing her glass of wine, she took a long sip to give herself time to think. *What was her mother's angle? Why was she pushing this so hard all of sudden?* She set the glass on the table and gave her mother her full attention.

"Mama. This is really coming out of left field. Why do I feel like you're *trying* to push me on Damon? Is it him specifically, or are you trying to tell me something?"

Her mother shrugged, clutching her own glass of wine between her fingers. "I'm just trying to help you out. You're in your thirties—in your sexual prime—and I don't want you to miss out on what could be the best time of your life just because you don't want to be in a relationship right now. I'm trying to look out for your vagina."

Seraph's jaw dropped open. "Hold on a moment.

Mama, are you suggesting that I *use* Damon… *for sex*?! The sweet boy that I babysat from the time I was fifteen until I left for college. Him?!"

Joyce regarded her with wide eyes. "I'm suggesting that you use *all men* for sex. Any man will do since they all have the same parts; he just happens to be in close proximity and already likes you enough to eagerly volunteer for the position."

Conveniently ignoring the part about Damon, Seraph jerked her neck back and sat up straight in her seat. "Oh, really? Did you use my daddy for sex?"

Joyce narrowed her eyes. "I sure did. Only, I messed around and got pregnant with you 'cause I was too busy screwing and wasn't paying attention to my ovulation schedule." She pursed her lips. "You were an accident."

Shrieking, Seraph jumped up from the table. "Mama, what the hell?!" Calling her an accident was a low blow, and Seraph didn't know if she wanted to cry or burst into laughter.

Her mother's stoic expression gave way when she exploded in a peal of laughter. "Uh-huh. That's what your smart ass get."

Desperately needing to escape the room where so many of her mother's words made her want to kick something, Seraph left the dining room and walked into the kitchen. She circled the room a couple of times until her head was clear—well, as clear as it could get—then returned to the table where her mother sat watching her with amusement written all over her face. She grabbed her glass of wine, lifted it to her mouth, and tilted it back, draining the remainder of its contents. When she lowered her head, she brought her eyes to a clearly tickled Joyce.

"I should just mind my business; huh, Mama?"

With a twinkle in her eye, Joyce smirked at her only child. "Yeah, that would be a good idea."

They finished their meal and carried their empty plates into the kitchen where they began to clean up. Once Seraph finished washing dishes, she turned to her mother who was wiping down the stove and counters.

"Mommy?"

Freezing, Joyce peered at Seraph over her shoulder. Seraph understood her reaction. It wasn't often that she called Joyce "Mommy". "Yes, baby?"

"Well, since I'm minding my business, can you mind your business too?"

Joyce gasped and dropped the rag she'd been using onto the counter, fisting her hands at her hips as she fought not to laugh. "Excuse me? I'm trying to help you *find* some business, little girl! All you do is work and go to brunch with your girlfriends."

Seraph frowned. "I happen to love my job, and I love hanging out with my girlfriends. Those two things make me happy. Is that so wrong?"

They stared at each other for a few moments before Joyce sighed and shook her head.

"No, there is nothing wrong with that. If you say you're happy then, as your mother, that should be my only concern." She dropped her hands from her waist and shrugged once more. "I suppose I just expect you to be more like me and need a little clitoral stimulation every now and then.

Seraph screamed. "Oh my God, Mama! You have got to chill out!"

Face twisted in confusion, Joyce raised her hands in the air. "What now? I thought we were speaking candidly. Is that not what we're doing? Did I get it wrong?"

Seraph laughed and crossed the kitchen to wrap her mother in a hug. "No, ma'am. You're not wrong; I just wasn't expecting that level of candor. It's fine, though."

Joyce leaned back and looked at her. "Are you sure?"

She nodded "I'm positive, Mama."

"Well, in that case, let me tell you about these adult toys I saw online since you don't want a man right now."

10
BARBECUE BOOTY

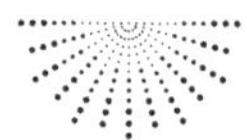

EVERY SPRING, JOYCE HOSTED A BARBECUE FOR FRIENDS and family. When Seraph was little, her father would grill and her mother would make all manner of side dishes. After he passed away when Seraph was twelve, Joyce assumed the grilling duties, and she taught Seraph how to prepare the sides. From then on, the two were a team, and Seraph looked forward to the barbecue every year.

Usually, she was a wonderful co-host, making sure guests were fed and enjoying themselves and keeping glasses full of tea and whatever other beverage they had on deck for the event. She was also a server, keeping dishes full, entertainment host, distributing cards and dominoes, and Don Cornelius, starting the Soul Train line.

This year, Damon's presence flustered Seraph. She

was on high alert, wondering what he was doing, if he was watching her, and most of all, if he was coming for her. Throughout the day, she bustled around her mother's backyard as usual but with a line of tension drawing her shoulders up to her ears no matter how much she laughed and danced or drank.

It was possible that she was being paranoid. Her mother's house was full of people, including Damon's father, Seraph's Uncle Louis. Surely, Damon wouldn't do anything outrageous with all of these people here. She tried to convince herself of that, but for some reason, the notion never took root.

At one point, later that day, Seraph noticed that both bowls of chips on the table were running low. She had extras in the house and figured she could pop right in, grab them, and come back out without anyone—Damon—noticing that she had gone. She rushed into the house and stepped into her mother's tiny, box-like pantry to find the half-empty bags of chips from earlier, and not even twenty seconds later, she felt him behind her. After two months of getting to know him intimately, his mere presence in the room made her body stand at attention, even if he was out of eyesight. This time was no different. There was no need to turn around, to call his name, to ask any questions. She knew without a doubt that it was him, and she also knew without question what he was there for.

Stepping inside the tiny room and pulling the door closed behind him, he pressed his nose against her neck and inhaled deeply. His proximity brought a shiver, and her fingers tightened into fists to keep from reaching for him. His hands came to her hips, the heat from his flesh warming her through her clothes.

"I went by your apartment last night. You weren't there."

Her lips trembled and a soft whimper escaped her throat as he lifted the hem of her dress in the front and eased his fingers beneath the elastic of her panties.

"I had a dinner meeting for work. Didn't get home until late."

Just as his index finger slid through her folds in search of the ever-present evidence of her arousal, his tongue marked a wet trail up the side of her neck until he reached her ear. He tugged her lobe into his mouth, nibbling as he used the wetness he'd found between her folds to play with her clit.

An involuntary shudder ripped through her body and Damon wrapped an arm around her torso in response. Bringing her body back against his, he added more fingers to the party, rubbing intently at the bundle of nerves to bring her to a quick release and kissing along her neck as she trembled in his arms, gasping his name as she came.

Without giving her a moment to think, Damon yanked her panties down and lifted her right leg, tugging her foot from the leg hole and resting it on one of the lower shelves in the pantry. He released his hold on her body for one quick moment—not even ten seconds—before grabbing her to him again and bending his knees to angle his hard dick at her opening, breaching her body in a slow intrusion that had Seraph moaning audibly, her head falling back against his shoulder.

Once he was completely inside of her, he pushed at her back, moving her upper body away from him and shoving her face to the wall, not caring that her cheek was smashed against the rough surface. He held her there with one hand and grabbed the back of her thigh with the other, keeping her open as much as he could in the small space as he stroked in and out of her quickly. Every drag of his veined dick against her ultra-sensitive, post-orgasm walls sent shockwaves of pleasure through her body, and Seraph found herself coming again, without even stimulating her clit, and holding her breath to keep from crying out loudly in the tiny box.

Her release was followed almost immediately by

Damon's, and he molded himself to her back as he emptied into her. They stood frozen like that for a minute before he pulled out of her and crouched down. In no time, she felt gravity do its thing, but before his ejaculate could start a slow drip out of her clenching hole, he scooped two fingers into her opening and stood, bringing them to her face and pushing his come-soaked digits into her mouth.

Greedily, she licked his release from his fingers, and once they were shiny and clean, he stepped back and tucked himself back into his pants, fixing his clothes in seconds, and wiping sweat from his brow. Heart pounding, she'd yet to pull away from the wall or even lower her leg from the shelf it was propped up on, and when she felt his eyes bore into the side of her face, she closed her own and sighed.

"I'm coming by your place tonight. Will you be there?" It was not only a question but also a demand.

She nodded and her nonverbal response must have been satisfying because he left the pantry, leaving the door open behind him.

Alone and able to think clearly about what had just happened, Seraph felt a wave of tears begin to rise up on the hem of shame. In the thirty-six years she'd been on this earth, she'd never had sex in her mother's home. Not as a teenager overcome with hormones, and not as an adult who lived with her mother until she'd paid off her student loans. The immediate high from endorphins was eclipsed by her dismay at what she'd done. Seraph lowered her leg, fixed her panties, and pulled her dress back down. She grabbed the two bags of chips she had gone into the pantry for in the first place and, with wobbling legs, exited the kitchen through the back door, grateful that no one seemed to have been in the house and heard her being debauched. In the backyard, she refilled the two bowls with the chips and tossed the empty bags into the trashcan she'd set near the side of the house before walking over to the swing and gingerly easing down next to Sierra. Her friend eyed her in amusement, a smirk flirting at the corner of her lips.

"Why are you looking all wild-eyed and frazzled?"

Seraph tried to give her friend a reassuring smile, but her lip trembled and the attempt fell flat. Eyes widening in concern, Sierra scooted closer to Seraph and dropped her voice to just above a whisper.

"What's wrong, Ser?"

Seraph shook her head. "Technically, nothing."

Sierra frowned. "I didn't ask for technicalities. I asked why you're sitting here looking shell-shocked." A thought occurred to her, and her eyes swept the yard quickly. She noticed Damon staring intently at them and quickly skirted her gaze past him before leaning into Seraph and asking, "Did something happen?"

Sighing, Seraph shook her head again. "Well…if you consider Damon fucking me in my mama's pantry something, then…yeah."

Sierra bent her neck to the side to get a better look at her friend's face. "You don't sound excited about it. I thought he was blowing your back out. You tired of him already?"

Another longsuffering sigh escaped Seraph's mouth, and she stood up, grabbing Sierra's hand as she did so.

"Come on."

Seraph led Sierra into her mother's townhouse and out the front door, down the path that led around the building to the driveway where she used her key to unlock her car.

"Get inside."

Once both women were inside of Seraph's car, Sierra stared at Seraph expectantly.

"Okay, you're scaring me. What is going on? Di—did Damon…rape you? Is that what happened? I swear to the Almighty that I'll kill him if he did. I'll put my cousin BoBo on it. He can make a man disappear, and no one would even know he's missing until it's too late. Say the word and Damon's ass is grass. Not even that good crab-grass that Auntie Joyce has in her back yard, but that weak shit, the yellow shit that they only plant on the poorer side of town and never grows no matter how much you water it. Just tell me; did he hurt you?!"

Seraph's lips twitched at the corner at Sierra's rant, but this wasn't a laughing matter in the least.

"SiSi. I don't know how to explain this. I feel like I'm addicted to really bad drugs. Damon *is* blowing my back out. Consistently. He made me come twice in that pantry. But…I—the thing is, I didn't want it."

Sierra stared at her. "You didn't want to have sex with him?"

Seraph shook her head. "No. Not at that moment and definitely not in my mama's fucking pantry. I'm not an exhibitionist; I don't get off on the possibility of people catching me in a compromising position. I —when I say I didn't want to, I mean mentally I didn't want to do it, but there was this…compulsion over me that overruled my brain. Like, I couldn't say no to him even though I wanted to." She sighed and leaned back against the headrest.

"It's been like that since the first time we had sex. The for real, penetrative sex. That shit at Jaime's party doesn't count because I woke up to frottage before he ate me out. But every time after we had sex the week following the party, I've been incapable of turning him down. He comes to me at work, at my house, here…he even fucked me in one of the cabanas at Lakeside Lounge. Everywhere and anywhere he wants. It's like…as soon as he says he needs me to come, I switch to autopilot then he can do whatever he wants to my body. I hate this but I can't fucking stop. Even now, I know he saw us leave the backyard, and I fully expect him to come bend me over right here in the front seat of my car while I'm parked in my mama's driveway. And I know, without a doubt, that no matter how much the idea mortifies me, I'll let him do it as many times as he wants.

The worst part of all of this is that Damon isn't the Damon he once was. Once we started having sex, the old him disappeared. He used to stop by my office to talk to me randomly throughout the week; he would compliment me on my outfits all of the time. Hell, he used to ask to hang out with the crew sometimes. Now? All he wants to do is fuck. The minimal amount of words he has for me is about fucking or him telling me how many more of my orgasms he needs. He's like a damn sex monster now. And, SiSi? I know I once said that all I needed was some young dick to put me to sleep and leave me alone, but now that I've got something similar, I can tell you that I want to go back in time and punch me in my face."

Silent tears trailed down Seraph's cheeks unchecked, and Sierra pressed a bunch of tissues into her hand, giving her some time to process her emotions without immediately bombarding her with the questions that arose as Seraph had spoken.

After a few minutes and a few more tissues, Seraph nodded and said, "I'm good."

"Okay." Sierra grabbed Seraph's hand and squeezed it. "Look, I know this is going to sound crazy as hell, but I need you to hear me out before trying to shut me down. Okay?"

Seraph blew her nose and then turned curious eyes on Sierra. "Okay…"

"I think that Damon might actually be a real—for real—sex demon."

Seraph stared at her for a second then started laughing. "Girl, what—ow!" The pain of Sierra squeezing her hand cut her off.

"You said you would hear me out, so hear me the fuck out. From what you just described of the interactions between the two of you and Damon's behavior in the past two months, it sounds eerily like the actions of an incubus. Incubi are male demons that have sex with women in their sleep. You said this all began when you woke up to him on top of you."

"Yes, but he was basically grinding his dick against my pussy. There was no penetration."

With pursed lips, Sierra frowned at her, annoyed that Seraph was once again interrupting her. "Non-penetrative sex is still sex, Seraph. Frotting is sex; tribbing is sex. What he was doing was sex. He was having sex with you in your sleep."

"But," Seraph stared off in the distance, "when I think about it like that, it sounds like something I don't want to name. Something that I would have never thought Damon could be capable of. Something that I never would have thought would happen to me. It sounds...bad."

"Because it *is* bad! Demons don't care about morals or consent, and they definitely don't care about how they make their hosts look! All they care about is getting to live free another day, and incubi do that by making their targets orgasm. It's like fuel for them. Without that fuel, they are weak and can be bound and cast out. It's why he fucks you so damn much. He literally can't survive without it."

Seraph's mouth fell open as so many things she'd questioned over the past ten weeks began to make sense.

"Oh my gosh," she breathed. "All this time I

thought he was strung-out on some kind of sex drug, and it turns out that he's—" Pausing, Seraph turned to Sierra. "What did you say he was?"

"Well, I said I *think* he's a sex demon. An incubus, to be exact. I think he's being possessed, but I don't know for sure."

"Okay. How do we find out for sure? And how can I get this damn...incubus...out of my life?"

Sierra's smile was an almost evil thing—caught between a scowl and a grin—and a little scary. "I know just the people you need to see."

11

THE REMEDY

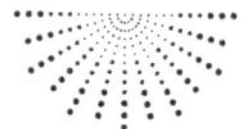

THE BRIGHTLY LIT STREET THAT SIERRA HAD BROUGHT Seraph to had surprised her. It had taken nearly a week for them to be able to go—for Damon to have a mandatory department meeting at work—and, from the subject matter that had brought them here, Seraph had expected something dingy and run-down; something… questionable. That wasn't at all what she found when they stepped inside of *Zing's Sweet & Sour,* a candy store nestled in between a furniture store and an old school arcade. On either side of the path that led from the entrance straight ahead to a long counter on the opposite end of the store were half a dozen short shelves filled with different kinds of candy.

Why had Sierra brought her to a candy store? Seraph wondered.

"Welcome to Zing's Sweet and Sour," called a gentle voice infused with something warm and soothing that made the tension in Seraph's shoulders slightly relax.

"Good morning, Zing," Sierra called back before grabbing Seraph's hand and pulling her toward the counter where a woman stood watching them, a soft smile on her face. As they drew closer, the smile shrank until it had disappeared completely.

Zing tilted her head at them, her hair—long locs twisted into two plaits on either side of her face—swinging forward as she did so. "Peace and blessings, sistahs. Tell me of the fear that brought you here today."

Seraph's eyes widened in surprise, but Sierra just nodded.

"I believe my friend," she gestured toward Seraph, "is being attacked by an incubus."

Before Zing could reply, the curtain of beads behind her parted and out stepped an older woman who looked so similar to Zing that Seraph did a double-take. They bore the same mocha-hued skin and thick locs that hung past where the eye could see, and they shared golden-brown eyes and a heart-shaped mouth. However, instead of the thin line where Zing's smile had once been, the older woman

—who was surely Zing's mother—wore a wide smile.

"Good morning, friends!" she exclaimed after hugging Zing to her side and pressing a kiss to her cheek. When she noticed Sierra, her smile stretched wider, and she came from behind the counter, locs that hung down to her ankles and were seasoned with gray flying in the wind as she pulled her into a hug.

"Sierra! It's so good to see you, dearest."

Seraph stepped to the side, her mind reeling as she watched their interaction. As close as she was to Sierra, she'd never known about her friend visiting this place with the strange but beautiful women and their odd phraseology.

"Sari," Zing called.

The older woman patted Sierra's cheek before looking over at Zing. "Yes, dearest?"

Nodding in my direction, Zing began, "She is in distress. The black chokes her."

All three women look at Seraph, and Sierra moved closer to her and took her hand.

"Mama Sari," she said, addressing the older woman, "this is my friend, Seraph. I believe she is being attacked by an incubus."

Mama Sari's brows knitted briefly, and then she pursed her lips and let out a soft, melodic whistle. A few moments later the curtains behind Zing rattled once more, this time parting to reveal a man ducking to enter the room. When he straightened, Seraph's eyes stretched as she took him in. He was *tall*—taller than the bead-covered doorway by several inches—with skin as dark as unrefined oil spurting from an untapped well. Rimless glasses sat perched on his nose above a salt and pepper beard that hung down to his chest, and his head was bald and shiny.

"My love," Mama Sari crooned, eyes twinkling with appreciation as she stared at the onyx giant who was surely at least seven feet tall.

His cheeks bloomed, eyes crinkling. "Yes, keeper of my heart?"

"I need Zing. Can—"

"Go. I have the store." Then, he seemed to sink nearly two feet into the ground behind the counter in one smooth motion.

Mama Sari grabbed Sierra and Seraph's hands in each of hers and led them around the counter where Seraph noticed that the tall man had sat on a stool, which made his immense height less visible from the other side of the counter. He smiled at her, tipping his head in the direction of the curtain with a quick wink. That small act worked to calm her somehow as she allowed herself to be pulled beyond the beads and down a narrow hallway into a room where she was ushered into one of four chairs that surrounded a round table.

"Okay," Mama Sari began after Sierra and Zing were both seated, "tell me how the angel acquired a demon."

Seraph looked at Sierra who stared back at her expectantly.

"Just…tell her what you told me."

With that, she did. Taking a deep breath, she focused on her fingers as she detailed the last three months, taking care to leave out the more explicit moments, just as she had done for Sierra. She told them how Damon's demeanor had completely changed and even though they were having sex, he felt like a stranger. When she finished speaking, she looked up from her hands just in time to see Mama Sari and Zing exchange a look she couldn't decipher.

Mama Sari smiled. "Well, friend, I have news. It is up to you to decide if it is good but know that it may not bring you much comfort."

Anxious and not at all looking forward to what the woman had to say, Seraph held her breath.

Reaching across the table, Mama Sari grabbed both of Seraph's hands in her own. "From what you have described, your Damon does have the characteristics of being possessed by an incubus. The possession likely took place during his time in New Orleans, which was just before the party where he initiated your first orgasm. Incubi are hellish creatures that must take a host in order to walk among the mundane. They thrive on sex, needing the hormones that are secreted during an orgasm to maintain a tight hold on their host. They tend to attack their victims at night, as we are all most vulnerable whilst we sleep, dipping into their dreams and presenting an irresistible interaction." She paused and glanced at Zing briefly before returning her gaze to Seraph.

"Just about everything you mentioned is standard incubi activity…except for one thing."

Leaning forward in her seat, Sierra's lips parted. "What thing, Mama Sari?"

"Incubi are not known to pursue the same victim as consistently—*persistently*—as you have detailed. Night after night, they will attack scores of women to ensure that their hormone levels never fall enough for them to be cast out, but it has been three months for you. That is…puzzling."

"I—" the lump in Seraph's throat made swallowing difficult, but she had to push forward to give a final detail that she'd tried to avoid revealing. "Do you think it may have something to do with Damon being my cousin?"

Before Mama Sari could answer, Sierra piped up. "He's her *step*-cousin! They aren't related by blood."

Seraph glared at her friend. "That doesn't matter! I've known him since he was a small boy. He was raised by my father's brother, even after Uncle Louis and Damon's mother divorced. Blood isn't the only thing that makes people family." She turned back to Mama Sari. "Damon is my cousin."

"Friends, please. Emotions are high and your energy is angry. Please, calm yourselves."

"Calm ourselves?!" Seraph screeched as she pushed back in her chair, preparing to stand up and pace the room, her terror feeling too big for her to sit in it. "How am I supposed to remain calm when I'm getting fucked two-to-three times a day by a family member, and I can't even say no to him?! Please, Mama Sari, tell me how, because I am *desperate* to know!"

"All is well."

Seraph felt a hand on her forearm and gasped when she realized that Zing—who was previously sitting on the other side of Sierra—now stood in between the two of them. No sooner had she registered the thought did she release a breath she hadn't known she was holding, expelling all of the fear and hysteria that she'd felt suffocating her with every piece of information Mama Sari laid at her feet.

Suddenly, her head was clear and she truly believed what Zing had said. *All was well.* She looked across the table.

"Please forgive me."

Canting her head in acknowledgment, Mama Sari's smile never wavered. "All is well, friend. If it is your desire to eliminate the demon from your life, you must first bind him and then cast him out."

Seraph frowned. "If? Why *wouldn't* I want to get rid of a damn demon?!"

Mama Sari's lips stretched further into a grin that put all of her teeth on display. "Well, friend, there are many women who are looking for what this demon is giving you and might find your particular predicament enviable. However, it is not my position to judge; I am solely offering clarity and guidance."

When she realized what Mama Sari was saying, Seraph's face grew hot with embarrassment. She should have thought before she spoke. Of course, there were women out there looking for a man to give them consistently stellar dick without the emotional drama that often comes attached to a man. Hell, she and her friends had discussed the topic ad nauseam before she found herself in the crosshairs of a sex demon.

"Um. Right." She cleared her throat and straightened in her chair, giving the wise woman her full gaze. "Well...how do I get rid of the demon that is possessing Damon?"

"First, you must refrain from coupling for twenty-four hours. Then, you must—"

Eyes bucked, Seraph jerked her neck back. "Twenty-four hours?! That's a whole day!"

Sierra slapped her hands on the table and sat forward, face scrunched into a frown as she stared down her friend. "Girl, do you want to get rid of this demon or do you just want to complain about him but continue on as you have been?"

Pulled up short by the fire in Sierra's voice and eyes, Seraph settled back in her seat and lowered her tone. "Really, SiSi?" *Why did her friend sound so angry with her when she was the victim here?*

"Yes, really. I didn't bring you here to have you feign outrage over a situation where you expressed genuine fear to me. Don't insult Mama Sari or Zing that way. Either listen to what she's telling you or take your ass home and wait for Damon to show up and fuck you into a coma."

Seraph sucked in a breath through her nose, the mere thought making her nipples tighten beneath her t-shirt. When she put it like that...

"We understand that this may be a difficult decision for you, sistah."

Startled by the throaty voice, Seraph quickly

swung her head to face Zing. The woman sat in her seat with her legs crossed underneath her and a small smile curving her lips.

"It's not what you think," Seraph began, shaking her head. "I'm not hesitating because I don't want to give up the sex. I'm…scared I won't be able to make it that long because I'm physically unable to say no to him. As soon as he appears, I feel compelled to do whatever he is demanding of me. Even if I think that I don't want to, my mind is overruled by my body. It's a terrifying sensation to not really be in control of your body."

Zing's golden-brown eyes narrowed, and she looked at Mama Sari, who had already turned to face her. They stared at each other for a few moments, seemingly communicating silently, before Zing unfolded herself out of the chair and rounded the table to approach the floor-to-ceiling piece of solid wood furniture that looked similar to an entertainment center but was just glass-covered cabinets, multiple drawers of various sizes, and open shelves in the center of the piece. Zing opened a couple of different cabinets, removing a few items from each one, then returned to the table and dropped her wares in front of Mama Sari. The only things that Seraph recognized were the ball of twine, although it was a vibrant, deep-purple color instead of the usual off-white, and two twigs that were tied together. Mama Sari arranged the four items in a line in the middle of the table and looked at Seraph.

"Is it your desire to eliminate the demon from your life?"

Without blinking, Seraph nodded. "Yes, Mama Sari. That is my desire."

Mama Sari tipped her head once, and with one hand picked up the two misshapen sticks no longer than the width of her wrist and lifted the ball of purple twine with the other hand.

"Here is what you must do…"

12
THE FINAL FUCK

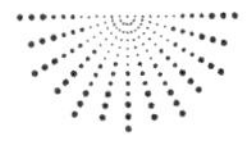

DAMON KNEW SOMETHING WAS UP WITH SERAPH.

He had to.

After she returned from *Zing's Sweet and Sour* with Sierra, she hid the items Mama Sari had given her in the bottom of a half-empty box of sanitary napkins in the back of her linen closet. It was an unnecessary precaution because the only thing Damon was ever interested in when he came over was putting his tongue on her clit and fucking her to the point of physical exhaustion. Still, she couldn't help her inclination to protect the items.

By the time Damon had arrived on her doorstep, she was fully convinced that he was what Sierra—and Mama Sari and Zing—had said he was. Seraph actually took some comfort in knowing that it wasn't her *little cousin* who regularly had her bent over the back of the couch but some random entity whose sole purpose was to make her come. This hadn't been *her Damon* who was dicking her down proper-like, trying to be the splackavellie she hadn't called for but couldn't turn away.

The knowledge was eerily calming.

Mama Sari hadn't been able to explain why the incubus occupying Damon's body seemed to have fixated on Seraph, but Seraph was just glad that it was the incubus and *not* Damon. It lifted a significant amount of guilt that she'd felt over the past few months and allowed her to simply enjoy what would hopefully be their last encounter together.

Maybe the shift in Seraph's attitude was what made him suspicious. Her usual attempt to talk him out of a night of hardcore, porn-worthy fucking was missing. Instead, she grabbed him by the hand and led him to her bedroom where she undressed him, admiring the hard planes of his body in a way she never really allowed herself before. When he stood before her, naked and ready with eyes narrowed in confusion, she eased him back onto the bed and began the first round by climbing atop him and settling her pussy over his mouth. He wasted no time in grabbing her hips as he licked her already-wet folds, darting his tongue in and out of her, mimicking the rhythm he planned to recreate with his dick.

She ground down on him, riding his face, no thought to whether or not he could breathe, simply chasing her own release, since they had that goal in common. His lips latched on to her clit, and her hips bucked automatically. Then, he sucked on that nub as if it was a triple-thick shake moving slowly through a straw, and that was all it took. Seraph gripped the top of her headboard as her thighs clamped around his head; she threw her own head back and released a keening cry as she came in his mouth.

While her body shook in the aftermath, Damon scooted from underneath her and came onto his knees. He pulled her hips back a few inches until she had to tighten her grip on the headboard so that she wouldn't fall face-first into the mattress and guided his dick inside of her wet warmth. Her grip changed from keeping her balance to holding on for dear life as Damon used every one of his glorious inches to stroke her at a pace that would likely knock her brain loose. She tried throwing it back at him, and he hit her with a thrust so powerful that she nearly crashed into the headboard.

Deciding on self-preservation, Seraph released her hold and pressed her face into the pillows, her toes curling as the new angle made his crown graze a different spot inside of her that was no less sensitive.

Damon followed her down to the bed, bringing his lips to her ear as he continued to fuck her steadily.

"What the fuck do you think you're doing?"

His warm breath danced across the side of her face and brought with it a shiver she couldn't escape.

"Wha—what you…*ooh*…mean?"

Biting her shoulder, he ceased his thrusting and began to grind into her. "Don't fucking play with me, Seraph. Something is different with you. I can feel that shit."

Even as her eyes rolled into the back of her head and her nerve endings jolted with each scrap against her spot, she lifted her ass, trying to take more of him. *"Damon,"* she moaned breathlessly. *"Shit."*

Momentarily distracted by her impending climax that he could probably feel approaching from inside of her, Damon grunted and shoved his hands underneath her body to palm her breasts, rolling her nipples between his fingers. "Uh-huh. Gimme that shit. Let it go."

Shoving her mouth onto a pillow, Seraph screamed through her release, the feeling of letting the sound out through her mouth somehow intensifying the feelings between her thighs. She came so hard that tears sprung to her eyes and she felt like she was melting into the mattress. As usual, Damon gave her no time to relish in her climax, quickly pulling out of her and flipping her onto her back before sliding back inside and returning to the power-fucking he'd initially employed.

He held her thighs open and thrust into her at a downward angle for several seconds before pulling out and shooting his release onto her gaping sex.

Panting, she stared up at him, wondering at the pinched look on his face as he pumped his dick and squeezed every drop onto her body. When he was done, he surprised her by rubbing his come into her skin, treating it like lotion as he massaged it into her belly and circled her nipples with wet fingers.

"Don't ever give my shit away," he rasped in a voice that sounded tight with barely controlled rage. "Your orgasms belong to me."

Seraph blinked up at him, slightly terrified of the dip in his baritone that sounded nothing like Damon's voice. It was clear that whatever was using Damon as a host was just there, under the surface of his luminescent skin, and the last thing she probably should be doing was needling the beast. However, knowing what she was dealing with, she couldn't keep the questions from falling from her lips.

"Why?"

He gave her a sharp look, brown eyes glittering as if a fire was burning behind them.

"Why what?"

"Why do my orgasms belong to you?"

"Because I need them."

Scooting up on the bed, Seraph pushed herself up into a sitting position and faced him.

"You always say that, but what does that mean? Why do you *need* my orgasms?"

A few moments passed while he stared at her in silence, his eyes narrowed as he observed her.

"Why are you asking me that now? Like you said, I always say that."

She pursed her lips, not swayed by his attempt at redirection. "I'm asking *now* because you've never smeared come on my titties and told me not to give *your* orgasms away." She swung her hand between the two of them. "This isn't a relationship, and we've never said anything about being exclusive, so when did my orgasms become yours?"

Grasping her ankles, Damon slowly pulled them toward him, spreading them on either side of his body until the loss of balance made her fall back against the bed and she was spread eagle in front of him.

"Your orgasms became mine when I started pulling them motherfuckers out of you like candy bars from a vending machine." Rising to his knees, he sank into her again, and her back bowed off of the bed as the sheer fullness of him made her breath catch in her chest.

Hooking one of her knees over his arm, he leaned forward and brought a hand to her throat as he began a slow grind into her warmth. With one hand, she grabbed his wrist and with the other, she grabbed his opposite bicep.

"Am I lying?"

Lost in the overload of sensations, Seraph didn't know what the question referenced, but she was quick to shake her head in hopes that it was the right answer. When he leaned down and flicked his tongue against her nipple before tugging the hard point into his mouth, she released a shaky breath and clenched around his dick.

"Do these orgasms belong to me?"

This time, she nodded but instead of rewarding her with attention on her other nipple, Damon squeezed the sides of her throat, using his fingers to apply pressure that made her instantly lightheaded. Combined with the way his dick was grazing her walls, the move had her ready to give up the ghost.

"Say it."

Her eyes popped open to find him staring down at her, expression dour as he worked her over.

"These are your orgasms, no one else's."

He stroked her harder but kept the same

agonizing pace. "Now, what's my fucking name?" His fingers increased the pressure on her neck, and her world felt hazy and magnificent. There was a ball of energy hurtling toward her, and she spread her arms wide to receive it. It crashed into her, and she splintered into a thousand pieces.

Gasping, she came on a gush of tears and a tsunami between her thighs. "*Damon*!"

13
THE BUDDY SYSTEM

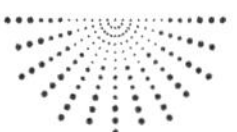

THE TWENTY-FOUR-HOUR SEX FAST BEGAN THE MOMENT Damon left Seraph's apartment. He waited until after she had awakened from another blackout orgasm and then saw himself out. She dragged herself into the shower to wash away the sweat and come that covered her body and then set a timer on her phone.

The next day, she made sure to stay out of her office while at work. Despite how late Damon had stayed at her house, she couldn't bank on him leaving her alone during the day and prevented another office session by inviting her department to work together in the conference room. Everyone had different projects, but the promise of a catered lunch and the opportunity to stretch their limbs were too tempting to pass on. It turned out to be a beneficial arrangement for all, with several people able to bounce ideas off of each other and brainstorm pitches. The culture in the sales department at NexTech differed from other tech companies in that it wasn't competitive in a toxic way. There was no value in undercutting each other or stealing clients or ideas. It was a family environment that fostered loyalty and passion for the job.

What had begun as a ruse to keep Seraph from being cornered by Damon turned into something that brought her real joy. She had almost forgotten about Damon completely until the urge to pee hit her after stuffing herself with food from Capital Grill. Halfway to the restroom, she realized that she was the only one in the hallway and her steps began to slow. Sweeping her eyes on either side of her, praying that Damon didn't pop up and pull her into one of the darkened offices, she was on high alert until she reached the multi-stall lavatory. The door swung shut behind her, and the sound of two women conversing made her sigh with relief.

She hurriedly emptied her bladder as she heard toilets flush and rushed to wash her hands so she could walk out with the women that she recognized from the advertising department, which shared a floor with sales. As she was rinsing the suds from her hands, she felt a stirring in her belly and the fine hairs on the back of her neck lifted.

He's out there.

"Hey. You okay, sis?"

Seraph dragged her blank gaze up from the sink to collide with that of one of the two women. One of her sculpted brows was hiked in the air, and even though a playful smirk was on her lips, her brown eyes were filled with undeniable concern.

Praying she hadn't been muttering aloud, Seraph asked, "Huh?"

The woman stepped closer, stopping just out of arms reach. "I asked if you were okay. You're staring into that drain as if you're trying to figure out how to jump into it." She chuckled, and Seraph swallowed hard, the reality that she would do just that if she could made her throat as dry as the desert in June.

"I—there's a man out there," she stuttered as she tried to figure out how to explain her dilemma, "a—and I—"

The woman's eyes narrowed, and she held up a hand.

"Say no more. You need help getting away from him?"

Seraph nodded so quickly that her teeth clacked against each other.

"We gotchu, don't we, YoYo?" She turned to the other woman who propped a fist on her hip and said, "We sure do. You're in sales, right?"

The first woman turned back to Seraph just as she was nodding a second time.

"I thought you looked familiar. What's your name?"

"Seraph."

"That's pretty." Touching her chest with the tips of her fingers, she said, "I'm Marissa," then she turned and hooked a thumb at the second woman, "and that's Yolanda. We're from ads. Come on, let's go." Moving closer to Seraph, Marissa yanked a few paper towels from the dispenser and held them out. Once Seraph dried her hands and tossed the crumpled ball into the hole between the two sinks Marissa looped an arm through hers and tugged her toward the door.

"Go first, YoYo, and hold the door. We have somewhere to be *right now*." She started laughing as YoYo pushed the door open, and Seraph was so caught off-guard that she began to laugh too, but it was short-lived when she noticed Damon leaning against the wall opposite the restroom.

One foot was bent behind him, balancing on the wall, with his arms crossed over his chest, and his eyes trained on her. As soon as they made eye contact, her pussy started weeping and her nipples beaded as if a strong breeze had washed over them.

Her steps slowed and she felt her chest begin to constrict.

Good lord, why did she think she could make it twenty-four hours? Just the sight of him had her ready to spread her legs in the middle of the hallway.

"You've been hiding from me," was all he said, face somber as if he had simply asked for the time. It might as well have been a siren's call, the way the low timbre of his voice had a physical effect on her, unlike anything she'd ever experienced before this thing began between them—before he came to her in the middle of the night all those weeks ago.

"I—"

Seraph was once again that marionette, drifting toward him unconsciously, magnetized to the power between his thighs—the magic that he created between *her* thighs. However, before she could even take a step in his direction she felt herself being yanked back into consciousness.

Marissa blinked at her in confusion before narrowing her eyes and tightening the connection of their looped arms.

"Girl, *we gotta go.*" She hadn't yelled but the emphasis on her words held a deeper meaning that Seraph was able to pick up on.

Nodding slowly, she blinked away the fog of lust

that had begun to settle over her mind. "That's right. We're on a bathroom break."

From behind, Yolanda let the door to the restroom swing close and placed a hand on both Seraph and Marissa's backs, guiding them toward the other end of the hallway. "Come *on*, they're waiting on us!"

The helpless look that Seraph wore wasn't an act. Damon rendered her completely incapable of making the right decisions, but she had these two women here blocking the invisible hold he had over her.

"I gotta go," she said apologetically.

"Okay." His response was simple, but Seraph knew it was anything but okay. "I'll be seeing you later, Seraph."

She licked her lips at his veiled threat and faced forward, leaning into Marissa as she turned the corner and reentered the main area of their floor.

"Where's your office?" Marissa asked her in a low voice.

Gesturing with her chin, Seraph steered them to the right. "We're working out of the conference room today."

The three women made their way through the maze of cubicles until they reached the glass wall of the conference room where several people were sitting in cushioned chairs at odd intervals around the oblong table. Some were pouring over papers while others typed away on laptops. Nearly everyone wore headphones or wireless earbuds as they worked. Seraph pulled her arm from Marissa's and turned to the two women to thank them when her eyes collided with Damon's. Maybe it was her bewildered expression or the way she gasped when she saw him, but Marissa didn't even hesitate. Instead of turning to see what—or who—caused Seraph's reaction, she reached around the woman and opened the door of the conference room and pulled her inside.

Seraph blinked rapidly and led them to the section of the table that she had commandeered. Taking a seat, she pulled her laptop toward her and watched as Marissa sat and grabbed the sheaf of papers sitting alongside the computer. She turned to Yolanda.

"YoYo, go on to our department, but keep an eye on him and text me when he leaves. That's when I'll come out."

Yolanda nodded and started for the door, but Seraph grabbed her hand and squeezed it.

"Thank you, Yolanda. You didn't have to do this, but I appreciate it more than you know."

The other woman shook her head. "Nah, sis. I *had* to. We have to look out for each other because if not us, then who?" With that, she left the room.

Releasing a heavy breath, Seraph shook her head. "I'm a fucking mess."

With a sharp tap on her forearm, Marissa got her attention. "No, ma'am. None of that. You're strong and will get past this."

Seraph chuckled humorlessly, keeping the sound low so as not to attract undue attention from the rest of her team. "You wouldn't say that if you knew why I was avoiding him."

Marissa stared at her for a moment, and then asked, "Do you want to talk about it?"

Glancing around the conference room, Seraph checked for any inquiring eyes and found none, but she couldn't shake her paranoia. Leaning forward, she dropped her shoulders.

"You probably think he's beating me or something but—"

"Girl, that man could be harassing you about a stapler for all I care." Marissa leaned closer and dropped her voice until Seraph had to strain her ears to hear her next words. "I know fear when I see it, and the look I saw on your face—in your *eyes*—when you were at that sink was all the explanation I needed to make a move."

A muffled buzzing sounded, and Marissa sat back in her seat, reaching into the neckline of her shirt and retrieving a cell phone. She stared at the screen for a second then looked up at Seraph.

"He's gone."

Before she could say anything else, Seraph grew overcome with gratitude and wrapped her in a tight hug, whispering, "Thank you," into her ear. When she pulled back, Marissa gave her a hard stare.

"When he said that he'd see you later…was that the threat it sounded like?"

Seraph cringed. The way those words had rolled off of his tongue and the knowledge of what he meant by it made her loins quiver. "It definitely was, but not like you think. Don't worry, though. I'm leaving early and he has no idea where I'm going. He won't be seeing me later at all."

Marissa pursed her lips. "Okay, but that's just for tonight. If this guy is seriously a problem then maybe—"

Reaching over, Seraph grabbed Marissa's hands over her cell phone and squeezed them. "He's not a serious problem. Not really." She squinted as she thought about it. "I mean…*he is,* but not like you think. It's just—" Breaking off mid-sentence, she shook her head and squared her shoulders, looking Marissa straight in the eye. Rambling would not get her point across.

"Look. I am incredibly grateful that you're concerned for me, and I could never repay you for how you came through for me back there. I just need to get through tonight without running into him again. That's my only priority right now. I can't even think about tomorrow or the next day."

She didn't look happy about it, but Marissa sighed and nodded, pulling her hands from Seraph's and lifting her phone into the air.

"Okay, I hear you, but I'm going to worry all night unless I hear from you, so you need to pull out your phone and program my number. I'd love for you to text or call me tonight and let me know you're somewhere safe."

That was an easy concession for Seraph to make. She lifted her phone from the table and navigated to her contacts so that she could input Marissa's information. Once she had her locked in, she sent off a text and watched as Marissa saved her number into her phone as well. They hugged once more, and then Seraph waved as the other woman exited the conference room and pulled the door closed behind her.

Everything she'd said to Marissa had been true. She needed to get out of that building and across town as soon as possible. Nothing else mattered except that because she couldn't afford to start her twenty-four hours over again. Her phone buzzed and she glanced down, expecting to see something from

Marissa but was instead greeted with a text from Sierra, informing her that she was in the lobby and on her way up to Seraph's floor.

It was almost time.

14
CURSEBREAKER

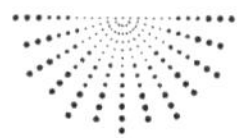

THE DAMON FROM BEFORE HAD NO IDEA WHERE ANY OF Seraph's friends lived, so it made sense for her to stay with one of them while trying to avoid him. Since Sierra was the only one privy to the entire ordeal, her home was the best choice. It didn't hurt that she also had enough knowledge of the... otherwordly things that Seraph had to do to ensure she didn't accidentally bring something else to life while trying to get rid of the incubus.

Switching her phone to silent mode wasn't enough because the myriad of vibrations from Damon's constant phone calls was distracting her, but shutting the device off completely wasn't an option because she was watching the timer intently, waiting for that twenty-fourth hour to be upon them. At 1:47 a.m., she powered down her phone and left it on the nightstand in Sierra's guest room before joining her friend in her attic. Devin had built Sierra a mini armoire that she used as an altar. Sierra had insisted that it was the perfect place for the task because the atmosphere surrounding her altar was already conducive for convening with the spirit world.

Seraph simply took her word for it and sat in front of the three-foot structure with her legs folded underneath her. The four items she'd purchased at *Zing's Sweet and Sour* were on the altar in front of her, waiting to be utilized.

A ball of purple twine.

Two twigs wrapped together.

A palm-sized gray rock with a piece of vine attached.

A slim box that held two white matches.

Running the steps in her head on a constant loop, Seraph grabbed the matchbox and retrieved one match. She struck it on the side of the rock and held the flame to the tip of the vine. When the vine caught fire, it retracted, curling up until it reached the end, in the center of the rock. That's when purple smoke began to rise from the rock, and it was Seraph's cue to start the next step.

She unwrapped the two twigs and grabbed the ball of twine. Holding the twigs perpendicular to each other, she began looping the twine around them while repeating a chant out loud.

Bind this demon, break his hold.

Cast him out, destroy his mold.

Free his host, release his soul.

Clear his mind, make him whole.

Seraph repeated the chant seven times while steadily wrapping the twine around the sticks. She worked slowly, being careful to follow the exact pattern that Mama Sari had demonstrated for her. When she finished the seventh round, she used a pair of scissors Sierra handed her to snip the twine then laid the wrapped sticks on top of the rock, directly in the center of where the smoke was emitting. The smoke grew thicker until she could no longer see the sticks, so she pulled out the second match, struck it, and tossed it into the smoke. The flame grew, burning brightly for seven seconds before snuffing out completely, taking with it the smoke, and leaving an empty rock sitting on top of the altar.

15
HER DAMON

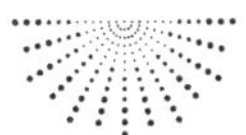

After the ritual, Seraph climbed into bed, but rest didn't come easy. Seraph tossed and turned for hours, her mind racing with scenario after scenario, her nerves at the outcome plaguing her well into the morning. At five, she cracked open her laptop and shot off an email to her boss, letting Gina know that she elected to work a half-day and would be in the office by noon. Gina emailed her back within two minutes, her reply consisting of a couple of thumbs-up emojis and a short "No problem". Satisfied that her job wouldn't miss her, she fell into a fitful sleep.

What felt like minutes later, Sierra burst into her room, jolting her awake. Seraph scanned the room with wide eyes, her heart pounding. Finally, she blinked blearily at Sierra who stood over her exasperated, as if she had been calling Seraph's name multiple times and was annoyed by the lack of response.

"What's going on," she asked groggily.

"Ser, turn on your damn phone! Damon has been rushed to the hospital!"

"Huh?" Pressing the heels of her hands to her eyes, Seraph shook her head, certain that she had heard Sierra wrong.

Sierra yanked the cover off of the bed and dropped a pair of jeans and a t-shirt onto Seraph's legs. "You heard me. Get dressed. Auntie Joyce has been calling me since she can't get a hold of you."

Finally understanding what Sierra was trying to say, Seraph jumped out of bed and threw on the clothes. She rushed through brushing her teeth and emptying her bladder then followed Sierra out of the house to climb into the passenger side of her friend's car.

"What happened?"

"Apparently, he was hit by a bus in front of your office building."

Seraph twisted in her seat to stare at her friend, mouth gaped open in horror. "What?!"

Sierra nodded, her hands gripping the steering wheel tightly. "Yeah. It was on the news. Someone in the building saw it happen from a fourth-floor window. Said he walked right off of the sidewalk and was immediately struck by a Metro going forty miles per hour. The bus didn't even have a chance to brake or swerve."

"Oh, my God!" Bringing her hands to her mouth, she swung her gaze to the windshield, staring blankly at the pavement as she thought about the ritual she had completed not even twelve hours ago.

"Do you—" she paused when Sierra's eyes quickly flickered over to her before returning to the road. "Do you think this has something to do with the binding?"

Sierra pursed her lips. "Absolutely."

Although Seraph was expecting that answer, it didn't make the heavy feeling in her chest go away. She was at a loss for words and they rode the rest of the way in silence. When they arrived at the hospital, they ran into the relatively empty emergency room where Seraph instantly spotted her mother and her Uncle Louis standing at the reception desk.

"Mama!"

Joyce spun around at the sound of her name and burst into tears when she saw Seraph. Seraph ran toward her and wrapped her in a tight hug.

"It's Damon," Joyce sputtered through her tears, her voice muffled by Seraph's shoulder.

Seeing her mother in tears sparked her own, and Seraph began crying as well. A heavy hand fell to her shoulder and she turned as her father's brother pulled her into a hug. She wrapped her arms around him tightly. "Is he okay? Tell me that he's okay."

Her uncle released a shuddering breath and stood back. "We don't know yet. I'm up here looking for answers right now." He gestured at the desk and the nurse who sat behind it with a sympathetic moue.

Joyce touched her arm. "They told us that he died at the scene."

Seraph gasped, her hands flying to her face, a fresh round of tears spilling from her eyes. That heavy feeling in her chest settled even deeper and her breaths became short.

This was her fault.

"But the paramedics resuscitated him," Joyce continued. "He was life-flighted over here, and now we're waiting to hear from the doctors." Her words were like a summons because as soon as she finished speaking, there was a high-pitched buzz followed by a door swinging open on their right.

A man wearing blue scrubs walked out. Both Louis and Joyce rushed toward him with Seraph and Sierra following closely behind. The older pair began shooting off rapid-fire questions, barely giving the man a chance to speak. He was apparently used to it because he stayed calm and expertly maneuvered into the conversation, providing answers that made Seraph's head spin and gut clench.

Severe swelling in the brain. Coma.

Seraph instantly recalled the words Mama Sari had spoken after explaining the ritual to her.

"Prepare yourself, friend. The host must die for the incubus to be cast out."

She'd heard the words, loud and clear, had processed them, and understood what they meant. But standing in the waiting area of the emergency room was a shock to her senses. Shaking her head in disbelief, she walked away from her family and slumped into a chair. "This is all my fault."

"No, it's not," Sierra immediately countered, having followed her over to the sitting area. "I'm not going to let you beat yourself up about this. Yes, you performed a ritual to bind and cast out the incubus, but you had to do that to protect yourself. All of this," she waved her hand around the waiting room of the hospital, "is the fault of whoever gave that thing entry to Damon's body. I know you probably don't want to hear this right now, but it's more than likely Damon's fault."

Eyes narrowed, Seraph looked at her friend in disbelief. "What?!"

"Girl, listen. We've *been* telling you that Damon liked your ass, and then suddenly, he is possessed by a demon that wants to fuck you night and day? That is some kind of coincidence."

Seraph sat in silence, her mind once again going a mile a minute. She couldn't deny that there was something to what Sierra was saying. Even Mama Sari had been confused by Damon focusing only on her. *Had he let this happen on purpose?*

Getting an answer that day wasn't in the cards, and she soon found out that Damon had been put in a medically induced coma while his body temperature was dropped in an effort to reduce the swelling in his brain. The doctors said he could have visitors, but Seraph refused to go in. She told her mother and uncle to take all the time they needed because they had a stronger relationship with him, but the truth was that she was scared.

She was completely terrified that she would walk in that room and the man in the bed would be the one she thought she'd gotten rid of. *What if she had gone through all of this just for none of it to work? What then?*

Her refusal to see Damon was an afterthought as his mother finally arrived from Dallas, along with her husband and their young children. Seraph was forgotten as her uncle and mother spent the time bringing the new arrivals up to date with Damon's condition. She took that as her opportunity to slip out unnoticed, riding with Sierra back to her house where she gathered her things and drove herself home to her apartment.

Damon was in a coma for three days following the accident, and on the third day, Joyce declared herself sick of Seraph's excuses and personally picked her up from her apartment and drove her to the hospital.

"I know you're scared to see him like that, but you can't abandon him, baby. He needs to hear from you."

With her arms wrapped tightly around her waist, Seraph willed the headache she felt forming to give up the ghost and back down. She'd had to hear too often about Damon's *needs* over the past three months and even though it was in a different capacity, she couldn't help the way her body reacted to it. Damon, or the demon, had trained her well and she hated it.

When they reached the hospital, they signed in at the nurse's station, pressed their visitor stickers to their chests, and Joyce led Seraph to the room that Damon had been moved to. They stepped inside the room just as a nurse was completing a check on his vitals. He greeted them with a warm smile and encouraged them to talk to Damon and hold his hand. Before he left, he showed them how to call them at the desk if anything happened then stepped out of the room, pulling the door closed softly behind him.

Seraph stood near the door, staring at the wall, completely disregarding the occupied bed taking up the majority of the space in the small room. Joyce pulled one of the plush armchairs over to the head of the bed on the side with no machines, and then she grabbed Seraph by the arm and pushed her into it.

"Talk to him," she instructed.

Staring at her mother helplessly, Seraph asked, "What do you want me to say?"

"Anything!" Joyce threw her hands up in exasperation. "Talk to him as if nothing happened. Talk to him about whatever you two would talk about before. Be normal. He needs that right now. He needs to know that we are here for him."

Seraph sat there silently for a moment. Again, with Damon's needs. "Damon and I didn't really talk." Her face heated as soon as she'd said the words, thoughts of the things they did *instead* of talking running through her mind. But...wasn't that why they were all here in the first place?

Smirking, Joyce propped a hand on her hip. "Mmhmm. I bet. Then why don't you talk to him about what y'all were doing in my pantry at the barbecue last month?"

Mouth hanging open in shock, Seraph watched her mother tilt her head toward the bed then walked out of the room. She'd known it was a possibility that someone had heard them, but finding out that her mother had known this whole time was mortifying. It also explained why she continued to suggest that Seraph and Damon get together; she probably thought they already were.

Bending over, she balanced her elbows on her knees and pressed her face into her hands, listening to the hum and beep of the machines that worked to monitor the man who lay still beside her. Faintly, she could hear him breathing, and it occurred to her that she'd never experienced him sleeping beside her. He always left immediately after he deemed them finished. It was just one more factoid in the long list of fucked-up shit she'd endured from him.

She sat there, wrapped up in her thoughts until finally, her curiosity got the best of her, and she took a peek at him.

And immediately, she regretted it. Her eyes filled with tears as she took in his appearance. His face was swollen and mottled with purple and black bruises. His arms were covered in cuts and scratches. There was a cast covering his right foot that stopped in the middle of his calf, and a long gash covered in sutures across his forehead that would more than likely become an undeniable scar. It would be an ever-present representation of how he had once possessed her while simultaneously being possessed.

Suddenly, she was filled with rage.

"I hate you for this," she whispered in a gritty, anguished voice. "*You* did this. You terrorized me for months and yet, I'm being pushed to be here for you. It's not fair. You took and took *and took* from me—without ever asking if it was what I wanted—but I'm supposed to care that you got yourself hurt? You're the dumbass who stepped into a busy street, probably on the way to find me and fuck me senseless—" Her voice cracked and she stood from the seat, pacing the room for a moment before returning to the chair and slipping her hand underneath his. She curled her fingers up to thread them through his limp ones, clutching his hand in hers. She was angry, yes, but this was still Damon—maybe even *her* Damon.

"Why did you do this? If you liked me, why didn't you just say so? Why put us through all of this? I can never look at you the same; you know that? I don't even know who you are anymore, but after the things you've done to me, I don't know that I want to go back to how things were before. I think it's best if we sever all ties completely." Even after getting that off of her chest, she still didn't feel better, but as she sat there, she had another thought.

"Damon. When you wake up, you'd better be your old self again because you are out of your damn mind if you think I'm about to climb on this tiny-ass hospital bed and bounce on your dick." It was funny because she knew that he was in no position to do that, but it was right up the incubus' alley.

"You know what?" She asked the quiet room, bringing her eyes to the man once more. "I just realized that with all of the fucking we did, you never kissed me. You ate my pussy and licked my ass but never kissed me in the mouth." She stared at his motionless body, wondering—no, *knowing* that she was crazy for the thought that crossed her mind.

The knowledge didn't change the desire, and she felt like she deserved it. She deserved the right to take something from him, no matter whether or not he wanted to give it. She stood from the seat, still holding his hand in hers, and leaned over him until she was hovering right over his face. Even with all of the bruises, it was clear that he was handsome, and four months ago, she would have even called him sweet. Now, she knew that he had the potential to harbor a monster inside of him. Still, she bent her head and pressed her lips to his.

Surprisingly, they were soft and moisturized.

Maybe his mother had been regularly applying lip balm on his behalf. She sighed into him, wondering how different things might have turned out if he had actually verbalized his feelings, but then she was surprised by the movement of his mouth under hers. What had felt like pressing her lips into the corner of her bent elbow, turned into an actual kiss with him responding. Her eyes flew open, and she was startled to find herself staring into Damon's eyes.

Lurching back, she broke their connection and tried to yank her hand free, but his grip was now ironclad and he refused to let her go. Her chest heaved as they stared at one another for a few seconds before the consistent beeping of a machine snapped her back to reality. She reached above his head to grab a large remote-like device from the wall and pressed the red call button. When the nurse responded in question, she breathed into the receiver, "He's awake."

16

ANOTHER AGAIN

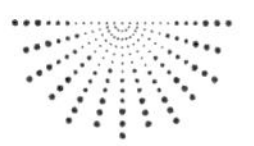

DAMON REMAINED IN THE HOSPITAL FOR ANOTHER three weeks after he awakened. When the doctor and nurse rushed in, they had to urge him to release Seraph's hand so they could begin testing. As soon as her hand was free, she shot out of her room and found her mother to let her know what was going on. Joyce called Louis, who showed up with Carla—Damon's mother—and her crew in tow, and they all camped out in the waiting room, eagerly awaiting word from the doctor.

The word came and brought with it shock and disbelief. Louis told Joyce and Seraph that Damon had retrograde amnesia. According to the doctor, Damon believed the date to be one that passed three months ago. When they repeated the date, Seraph's heart thundered in her chest. Damon thought it was the day of Jaime's Pajama Jam. *Why? What did that mean?*

Through a series of verbal tests, the doctors learned that while Damon hadn't sustained any injuries on that day, he'd been in New Orleans the night before and had gotten drunk on Bourbon Street with his friends before passing out in his hotel room. That's the last thing he remembered.

That was all Seraph needed to hear. She knew what happened after that. Hell, she knew what happened now. While the doctors were puzzled over his memory loss, Seraph knew what had happened. She'd chanted seven times for his mind to be cleared and apparently, it had. Once that realization settled in, she decided not to return to the hospital.

After endless tests, and scans, and examinations, the specialists that were called in couldn't figure out the cause of his memory loss and eventually decided to let him go home. Damon was released from the hospital and cleared to return to work on light duty. Except for a sprained ankle that would continue to heal over the next few weeks, no matter his location, he was in great shape. In fact, many people said that he was lucky—that being hit by a bus while on foot could have meant instant death. He was *lucky* to walk away with only a cut on his forehead, sprained ankle, and a few forgotten months. It sounded callous, but it was honest.

It was good news—the kind of news they could all use more of after hearing that he'd died at the scene. Instead of rushing to Damon's apartment with her family and his friends to celebrate his good health, however, Seraph kept her distance, on edge as she waited to see if he would do the inevitable and show up at her apartment, primed and ready to shove her face into the mattress.

It never happened.

As the second week following his release came to a close, she went through the motions of her nightly routine—plaiting her hair, selecting her clothes for work the next day, and getting ready for her shower. Throughout the entire process, she told herself that her constant sighing at regular intervals was because of the relief she felt at finally having some peace and in no way had anything to do with possible withdrawals.

Just as she stepped into the bathroom, she was startled by a hard pounding on her front door. It sounded like the police trying to beat her door in, and she rushed toward the front of her apartment, tugging on her robe and cinching the belt as she crossed the living room. Yanking open the door, her brows furrowed even as her belly leaped when she saw Damon standing on the other side, his face pinched into a frown with his eyes trained at the ground. He wore a pair of orange joggers and a black t-shirt that clung to a defined chest that she was well acquainted with. She noticed that he held his cell phone in one hand while his other was tucked into the front pocket of his loose jogging pants. The new scar across his forehead reminded her that it hadn't been that long since his accident, and she kept that in mind as she opened the door wider.

"Hey, Damon. What's going on?" She kept her voice light and comforting, hoping to ease whatever was on his mind that had his face scrunched the way it was, but inside, her body was buzzing at the sight of him.

His expression was impassive as his deep brown eyes rose from the ground, trailing slowly up her body from her bare feet until his gaze met her own, and she experienced a full-body shiver as if a gust of wind had just blown over her. The look itself wasn't exactly like the ones he'd given her recently, but it was still something more…intimate…than what she was used to from the Damon from…before.

"Sorry for popping up unexpectedly, but I haven't

seen you since I woke up, and I didn't want to discuss this over the phone."

Seraph swallowed against the lump in her stomach. That was shade that she'd have to let roll off of her back. He doesn't remember that they'd been here before. Although he was back to the Damon she'd always known, she couldn't help but be acutely aware of her nudity beneath her robe and the way he'd just ogled her didn't help. Even subtle, it made her anxious as her body responded in kind, preparing her for what usually came next.

Pulling the belt of her robe tighter and knotting it once more, she stepped aside to let him in. "It's fine; come on in."

He crossed the threshold with a slight limp in his step, and she wondered where his crutches were as she closed and locked the door behind him. When she turned around, he was sitting in the middle of her two-seat couch, his legs spread unnecessarily, taking up way too much space. Mentally, she knew that he was probably here for some arbitrary reason, but she didn't know how to act around him anymore. Just being in his presence spiked her temperature and made her pussy quiver, both inappropriate responses to someone who was essentially family—blood relation or not.

Completing the binding ritual and casting out the incubus was supposed to eliminate these feelings she had for Damon, yet they felt as prominent as ever. Her heart had begun beating at double speed the moment she laid eyes on him, and she felt sweat bead along her forehead as the temperature in the room seemed to go up a few degrees. *This was insane.* The man sitting on her sofa was *her* Damon; not the sex-crazed, orgasm-fueled monster she'd been spellbound by. She needed to get it together.

Clutching the lapels of her robe, she remained standing and leaned her hip against the back of one of the two armchairs in the room that faced the couch.

"So, what's up?"

"You kissed me."

The simple words were accusatory, and she should have seen it coming. It was the first thing he saw when he woke up and completely out of character for her, so, of course, he would remember. Closing her eyes, she dropped her head and shook it.

"Yeah. I did." She raised her eyes to meet his. "But I shouldn't have. It was wrong of me."

He stared at her unblinkingly. "Why'd you do it?"

"I—" She opened her mouth then quickly closed it. How did she answer that without divulging information that he never needed to know? "It felt like the right thing to do at the time."

He didn't respond to that, he just continued to stare at her for a long moment. Without saying another word, nor taking his eyes off of Seraph, he held out his phone. From where she stood, she could see that the screen was lit and, though confused, she moved to stand in front of him and pluck it out of his hands, being careful not to touch any part of his skin. When she registered the image on the screen, her jaw slackened and the blood drained from her face. And… maybe a part of her that she called herself burying deep down beneath propriety was turned on.

It was a picture—one that she recognized instantly—captured from Damon's point of view. Even though neither of their faces was in the shot, she knew, without a doubt, that the two bodies visible belonged to them. In the picture, Seraph was lying naked, on her back, hands cupping her breasts, fingers pinching her nipples, legs spread wide, with Damon's beautiful, hard dick lodged halfway inside of her body and his thumb lifting the hood of her engorged clit. She remembered how after the picture was taken, he'd later made her hold the phone in the air while he stared at it and simultaneously ate her pussy.

Slamming her eyes shut against the memory—and the sudden throbbing between her legs—Seraph clutched at the collar of her robe. She shouldn't pine for the time in that photo, shouldn't miss the freaky shit Damon had done to her while he was...not himself, but Lord help her she did. Barely a month had gone by, but instead of being grateful that she was no longer under attack, she was miserable. She could only say it in her head, but if she were being honest, she'd admit that she missed it—missed him.

However, the Damon in front of her was innocent and didn't know anything about that time, so she decided to feign ignorance.

"Uh, not sure why you felt like showing me some homegrown porn or nudes or whatever this is, but at least homegirl has some nice titties. Thanks? I guess." She tried to pass his phone back to him, but he refused to lift his hand and receive it, instead, nodding at the device.

"Keep scrolling. There is so much more than that one image."

She shook her head. There was no way she could continue looking at erotic pictures of the two of them and pretend to be unaffected. She could already feel her breaths shortening as her arousal started to set in. "I'm good, thanks. Here's your phone."

Stonily, he stared at her. "Do you think I'm stupid, Seraph?"

His gritty tone was so surprising to her that she took a step back. "Wha—what? I didn't—"

"Do you think I don't know what your body looks like? Hmm? All of the years I've spent watching you, wanting you, *craving you*—you think I don't have your curves committed to memory?"

"I—" She didn't know what to say, too busy trying to process his admission.

"You must think I'm dumber than a box of rocks. Why else would you look at this picture and try to play me like I don't know that's us?"

"Uh..." Taking another step back until her butt hit the chair, she sat down and folded her arms across her chest, putting pressure on her now aching nipples. *This* Damon was unfamiliar to her. With steel in his voice and in his eyes, he was neither the one she knew nor the one she'd known intimately, yet, she couldn't deny that he still succeeded at turning her on.

At this point, she'd forgotten what level of hell she was doomed to; she just kept sinking lower and lower.

"Damon..."

He shook his head. "Did you know, Seraph? Did you know how badly I wanted you? How I called you my angel, like your name, and used to pray for *my angel* to want me as I wanted her? But it never happened, no matter what I did. Then I woke up from what I thought was a hangover, only to learn that I'd lost three months of my life. *And then* I see this picture." His eyes narrowed in on her, and her breath caught in her throat. "Do you know that I was so desperate to call you mine that I let some crazy conjure woman in New Orleans convince me that she could help me?"

Eyes wide, Seraph shook her head. "What?!"

Damon leaned forward, planting his elbows on his knees and pinning Seraph to her seat with his stare. "You heard me. I went to New Orleans with Silas and Eric for their cousin's bachelor party, and while we were on Bourbon Street, an old woman approached me. She said I needed to come see her. I laughed her off, and me and the fellas kept moving, but then she said she could help me get the woman I loved to love me back, and that...well, those were the magic words. So, I followed her into some dingy shop off a back street and watched as she mixed up some weird concoction and poured it into a shot glass.

She told me that if I drank it, you would be mine, and I couldn't resist because I wanted you so bad—had been wanting you since I knew what it meant to crave something other than food—but you never looked at me twice, never acknowledged me. You called me your 'baby cousin' despite us not being related and even tried to hook me up with your coworker. With all of that shit on my mind, I didn't second-guess it before taking that shot glass of the unknown to the head. It didn't taste any different than a shot of Jägermeister, so I paid her and went back to Bourbon Street where Eric and Silas clowned me for the rest of the night. The thing is…that's the last thing I remember because I went to sleep that night after hanging out with my friends, but when I woke up, I was in a hospital room with you hovering over me, your eyes closed, and your lips on mine."

Seraph clapped her hands over her mouth, and her eyes filled with tears at the anguished look on his face. At the beginning of this whole ordeal, it never occurred to her that Damon hadn't known what was happening with his own body. When she was performing the ritual and chanting for his mind to be clear, at no point did she think about what it might be like for him once he was restored. But…as heavy as her heart felt on his behalf for what he was now experiencing, she reminded herself that he opened himself up to this. It was his obsession with having her that allowed the events of the last nearly four months to take place. He had no one to blame but the man in his mirror.

"You can't imagine how I feel, waking up, thinking it was just some accident, then learning that I'd lost three months of my life. Then to look in my phone, hoping for some clue about what happened, and see pictures of us—*of you!*—like *that* and not have any memory of it! That shit gutted me, Seraph. I'm tore the fuck up! So for you to look me in my face and pretend that it didn't happen is killing me right now."

His voice cracked on the last word, and the tears she'd held at bay fell unchecked down her face.

"Why would you lie to me about this?"

Shaking her head, she set his phone on the arm of her chair and wiped her face with both hands. Now was not the time to point fingers. "Damon…the…the thing between us—it wasn't good. You weren't yourself and it—" she cleared her throat, "it felt wrong. It *was* wrong. Everything about it terrified me."

Brows furrowed, he tilted his head. "What do you mean it felt wrong? That it terrified you? What does that mean?"

She didn't know how to explain to Damon that the sheer intensity of his focus on her over the past few months was terrifying. He'd had little regard for anything other than pulling as many orgasms out of her as was humanly possible and she hadn't been able to rest without fear that he would show up in the middle of the night and attempt to suck her soul out through her clit. Even more, there was no way for her to say that what terrified her the most was that she had become addicted to the way he that he always took her—despite her weak protests—without sounding crazy.

"It's just… you were doing a lot and I—I don't know how to explain it."

Silently, he stared at her, dark eyes seemingly peering past her flimsy excuse, before he pursed his lips. "Try me. Start at the beginning."

Sighing audibly, she rolled her eyes to the ceiling to avoid his gaze. She knew she needed to tell him; he deserved to know the things he'd done—even if it wasn't necessarily *him* doing them—but the thought of detailing his actions out loud embarrassed her.

"Well," she began, shifting in the chair and fixing her robe to better cover her thighs, "it started at Jaime's pajama party. You were flirting with me the entire night and didn't care that I kept shutting you down. I mean flirting heavy. You cock-blocked any guy I tried to talk to and even put your hard dick on my back. Then, that night, I woke up in the middle of the night with you on top of me." She hazarded a glance at him, his shocked expression calming her enough for her to continue. "You… did things to me."

"Did I… hurt you?"

Seraph heard the fear in his voice, heard the unspoken question, and rushed to reassure him.

"Not unless you count making me come until I pass out hurting me."

For the first time since arriving at her apartment, he sat back against the couch, running both of his hands down his face.

"Fuck!" he shouted. When he faced her again, his eyes were red-rimmed and face pinched tight. "What happened after that?"

Seeing how upset the information was making him, Seraph hesitated, but when he growled, "Tell me!", she continued. She told him what happened in her mother's kitchen and how he came to her home the same night. Avoiding his gaze, she ran through the list of every encounter they'd had from that first time up until the night two days before his accident. The only thing she withheld were her suspicions of him being possessed and the subsequent binding spell that she was one hundred percent sure had led to his memory loss.

When she finished, the effects of reliving the past few months were evident. Her heart was pounding, her pussy was throbbing and leaking wetness between her thighs, and her nipples were so tight that every brush of her robe against the turgid points was agonizing. And although Damon might not remember how intimately he knew her body, he still managed to take notice of her current state of arousal. He tilted his head to the side and eyed her through narrowed lids.

"So, that's what it takes, huh?"

Confused, she blinked rapidly and shifted once more, the action bringing his gaze to the hidden crevice between her thighs. Her body heated further under the intensity of his focus, and she fought not to shift again. Damn near six weeks without what had been daily for months had made her sensitive. A few choice rubs of her thighs together, and she was sure to come where she sat.

Eyes on her, Damon scooted to the edge of the couch.

"All this time I've been giving you hints that I was interested; trying to show you that I was ready and willing whenever you were—" he broke off on a mirthless chuckle, slowly rising to his feet. "Apparently, I was playing the wrong sport. I spent so much time pump faking, waiting for an opportunity to shoot my shot, when all along I just needed to steal my way to home plate."

He walked toward her, and Seraph's eyes widened with each determined step that he took, her knuckles pale from the death grip she had on her robe.

"I—" she swallowed thickly. "I have no idea what you're talking about."

Dropping down into a crouch in front of her, he smirked. "That's okay. I can show you better than I can tell you." Gripping the backs of her knees, he lifted her legs and pushed them up into the air. "Hands." Eyes glued to her glistening slit, he uttered the demand in a firm tone, and lightning quick, Seraph reached down and replaced his hands with her own, holding her legs in the air, keeping herself wide open for him as her breathing turned shallow. His eyes glittered with wonder and satisfaction and she felt herself clench involuntarily.

"Do you know how fucking turned on I was as I scrolled through those pictures?" He swiped a thumb through her wetness, eliciting a whimper from deep in the back of her throat.

Bringing his thumb up to his mouth, he sucked away her essence, and the look of euphoria on his face nearly unraveled her. "My dick was hard enough to split concrete."

He stood quickly, his hands going to the waistband of his pants, causing Seraph's stomach to clench in anticipation. And when he pushed the material past his hips, revealing an already steely erection that she knew *intimately*, she nearly bit a hole in her lip. She wanted him so badly that she was almost willing to beg, but then he stroked himself once, twice, before lining his tip up with her slit. She held her breath.

"Look at you," he murmured. She wrenched her gaze from his dick to his face, unable to hold in her whimper at the heated, hungry look in his eyes. "You're so greedy for this dick." Bending his knees, he dipped inside of her just a fraction before pulling back out. "Ignoring me for years but now you're about to cry if I don't feed you." He pushed in again and once more retreated after only wetting his tip.

Seraph's face contorted into a whine. She *was* about to cry. "Damon, ple—"

Before she could finish her plea, he grabbed his dick at the base and slapped her pussy with it. The pressure on her clit from the impact sent a zip of pleasure through her and she moaned.

"No," he bit out, voice clipped with restraint. "I'm running this." But then he contradicted his statement by sinking into her completely until his hips met her thighs.

Her eyes burned and she closed them tight as she fought to hold in her tears of relief. When Damon didn't move, she opened her eyes to find him staring down at her with an indecipherable look on his face. She opened her mouth to ask him what was wrong, but he pulled out and thrust forward roughly, causing her back to arch against the chair as his dick grazed her spot.

"Playing… these fucking… games… with me."

Damon muttered to himself as he stroked her with precision, gripping her hips and aiming for a spot inside of her that neither of them could see, yet both knew was there. And though this wasn't *that* Damon, maybe their encounters had embedded in his psyche like muscle memory because the way he twisted his hips and thrummed her clit sent her hurtling toward her climax just as quickly as ever. And while her stomach was still spasming and aftershocks continued, causing her pussy to clench around him, he quickly pulled out of her and tugged his pants up over his hips, slapping his wet dick against his belly. Then he yanked her onto her feet and pulled her down the hallway until they reached her bedroom. Once inside, he closed and locked the door before turning to face her.

With every step he took toward her, she took a step backward until the soft edge of her mattress knocked against the back of her thighs.

Waiting, she stared up into his dark brown eyes,

the intensity of his gaze nearly overwhelming her. When he reached up, she expected him to grab her breasts or lift her onto the bed, but he surprised her by framing her face in his hands and lowering his mouth to hers. She clutched at his waist as he moved his mouth against hers, licking along the seam of her mouth until she opened for him. Their tongues touched and a whimper rose in the back of her throat as her knees weakened. Lifting her hands from his waist to his forearms, she held on for dear life as he painted the inside of her mouth with his distinct flavor.

When he pulled back slowly, dialing the kiss back to small nips and licks, she chased him without a shred of shame, pushing up on her toes and stretching her lips toward him, not wanting to let go of the feeling that he'd ignited inside of her. His low chuckle made her eyes pop open, and her heart skipped a beat at the sight of those twin dimples. Oh, how she'd missed seeing them on his smiling face. Their appearance—along with the kiss they'd just shared—was another indicator that the Damon standing in front of her was different. *This* was the right Damon.

He pulled her robe from her shoulders and tossed it to the ground before grabbing her at the waist and hefting her onto the bed. Then he moved back a few steps and disrobed, dropping his clothes into a haphazard pile at the base of her bed. And as he stood there, completely nude, slowly stroking his still hard dick, his eyes on hers, bottom lip tucked neatly between his teeth, her mouth watered, pussy clenched, and she thought that maybe *she* was the one who was possessed after all.

ABOUT THE AUTHOR

Chencia C. Higgins is just a girl from Texas writing about sassy, southern women finding love. With a multitude of titles under her belt, she has made it her mission to create stories in which Black women are loved out loud. In 2019 she won a Romance Slam Jam Emma award for her debut paranormal romance, Janine: His True Alpha. When she isn't hunkered down in her writing cave, Chencia can be found with her nose in a book (or two, or three), saving recipes on Pinterest, and traveling as much as possible with her family.

To be informed about future releases, events, and happenings, visit her website and join her mailing list.

www.therealchencia.com

http://eepurl.com/dhCDsz

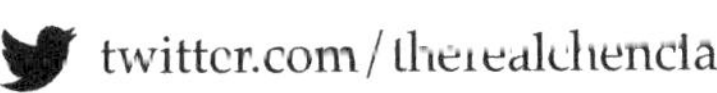
twitter.com/therealchencia

instagram.com/ohchencia

BB bookbub.com/authors/chencia-c-higgins

Made in the USA
Middletown, DE
30 June 2022

68081902R00099